ONCE I WAS KING

~ Novel ~

Corinne Wandenburg

Motto:

"... your Highness arrives too young into a very old world ...!"

~ Joao Chagas ~

To Manuel Reis, with respect and friendship !

Infarom Publishing

office@infarom.com
www.infarom.com

ISBN: 978-973-1991-67-2

Publisher: **INFAROM**
Author: **Corinne Wandenburg**
Translator: **Maria Letiţia Chiculiţă**
Correction editor: **CarolAnn Johnson**
Cover design: **Liping Wang**
Original title: *Am fost odată rege* (Romanian)

CHAPTER 1

Nothing in the world is more beautiful than the first season of the year. Everything revives, the birds are flying, looking for the reasons for a new beginning of creation, which they were meant for. The grasslands are blooming, the trees rustle again, because, you see, reader, they have leaves again. I think that people who were born in spring are blessed because they can rejoice naturally without realizing it, in the sun, the light breezes, the wonder of walks in the fresh air. Maybe people who were born in spring are more optimistic, more confident and, you see, more blessed.

I cannot possibly know that, for I was born in late summer, when everything is completed, when one knows that the cold will settle in one or two months later. But I don't know whether the Portuguese have felt as dramatically the passage from the warm weather to the cold weather and the other way around. In Portugal, it is always warm. But who knows what sadness presses on them with all that incessant heat. For certain, gray thoughts eat at them, or else they wouldn't have sung all those sad songs, almost like mourning, which they always murmur when they get together. And they do like to gather together, masses of them, and sigh over their life in the *fado* rhythm. I believe that every people have a special song in their hearts, in a rhythm that belongs strictly to that particular people. It's easier with a song; sometimes, poetry lifts you up to another level which you are not always capable of grasping, of understanding and accepting. That is why it is so much simpler with a song. Drama is already too complicated.

Portugal, this country at the edge of Europe, from where, if you take a step and close your eyes, you find yourself in the New World – America – is an fascinating land with a special, fairy-tale charm of its own. But we've already wandered too far from the subject of this book. If you like Portugal, or if you are at least curious about it, you may begin to satisfy your curiosity by reading the pages of this book, which shows or at least tries to, why the Portuguese carry all the time in their subconscious, a feeling of sadness, and in the end, maybe you will come to understand their music, their *fado*.

The theme of this book is a sad page from the history of this beautiful country, but because of the main character, also gives a reason to smile. It is like the music, sadness that brings happiness. This may sound like a contradiction, but in the case of this people full of sun, it is a reality lived hour after hour.

Why Portugal again? I don't know what to answer to something that comes from deep down in my soul and obviously has no explanation. Anything that comes from love and passion of any kind does not deserve meaningless words. I love this country and its people, its vineyards, its monasteries, but I especially love its history, from which I bring to the surface excerpts that I mold and dress in the mysterious silk that I weave in my heart.

If, in one of my previous writings, I spoke about the wonderful and mysterious *Infanta* Catarina de Braganza, whose father brought Portugal back to the Portuguese, why couldn't we talk in these pages about the last King of this country, a king by accident and for so short a time, who understood, even in exile, to preserve his charm and optimism and to sing his sadness like a true Portuguese with a smile on his lips. Who other than Manuel II made me take up the pen and start writing? One needn't be Portuguese to love Portugal and the House of Braganza; one needs only to listen to their songs when they gather together. More people gathered together means, inevitably, *fado*. It means laughing and crying at the same time; it means everyday life in lands that do not know what winter with a temperature below zero is, but which know the waters of the ocean and the sea.

Try to get to know ordinary people, for they are wonderful and benevolent, and in some respects, they are pure and innocent. The book is not about them, however, but about the young King, born in the spring on the banks of the Tejo River.

4

CHAPTER 2

May God bless King Joao V who ordered the Belem Palace built in 1726, for it is he that we are talking about. He wanted the palace to belong to the Crown and the monastery to be moved there. What a beauty, what a masterpiece of the architects of that time! The palace, situated on the shore of the Tejo River, on a hill that provided it with magnificent grandeur, gave a moment of joy for any mortal passing by Belem, with or without the intent to enter the Jeronimos Monastery nearby. It was of solid construction which resisted even the powerful earthquake that destroyed Lisbon in 1755. With a few small repairs, that Baroque palace stood high on its hill, watching through its windows as Lisbon shuddered helplessly into ruins. The capital was slowly, gradually, rebuilt, and calm settled over the city. Tejo, witness to it all, remained silent, carrying its undulating waters to the shore, stating its indifference in its subdued sound. That lovely palace witnessed many events in history, more or less important, but its walls do remember one in particular.

One spring, which is so lovely in Portugal, rumor had it that a new natural king was born. And that was true. Indeed a prince was born on the 19th of March, 1889. He was not the firstborn son, so he had no reason to fear that he would have to carry the burden of the crown, but to his parents he was a guarantee of their continuity and a hope that life prevailed, as they remembered the sad event that had occurred only one year before, when the first girl, *Infanta* Maria Ana, was born and died shortly after. But let us go into the story.

In the apartment of Duchess Amelie de Orleans, there was a big hustle and bustle on that happy day. Doctors were crowded around her and the child, who, may God be praised, was crying lustily, a sign of healthy lungs. The Duchess, still feeling weak, was lying in bed, watching all that activity from the room where she was trying to regain her strength for the announced visit of the Prince. Her maids were arranging her and gathering everything that needs to be gathered after a birth. The windows were wide open because the weather was already pleasant, and they needed the fresh air to enter the room. The servants finished everything quickly, and the baby was handed over to his mother. Maybe Carlos, her husband, was supposed to see her like that, who knew?! Only the nurse stayed in the room, in case anything was needed. The Duchess knew that they would soon take her little boy so that she could get some rest. A servant on the other side of the door suddenly opened it and announced:

"Madame, your husband, the heir prince!"

Amelie held her child closer and dismissed the nurse to the adjoining room. Carlos entered joyfully and knelt down by the bed. He took his wife's hands and kissed them happily.

"My dear, thank you, you gave us one more son for ourselves and for Portugal. The doctors say he is in good health, and that you are well, too, only you need to rest. I ordered nineteen cannons to fire on the bank of the river to celebrate another heir. You will certainly hear them. I have also thought of a name for our son, a famous name, of a king in the ancient history of our country. We shall call him Manuel! What do you think, my dear?" the loquacious prince asked his wife.

"It is a good name, my dear, beloved husband," Amelie answered. "But we have to choose the other names as well."

"Don't worry, we shall choose them together. Today I am ecstatic! If you feel able, listen to the cannon fire; if not, then sleep and regain your strength, which is a good thing, I think. Ah, I almost forgot," said the prince who started searching for something in his pocket. He found it and started laughing. He kissed Amelie on her tired forehead and put a small ring on her finger, his gift for the gift she gave him.

The Duchess smiled, looking drowsy. Carlos understood and called the nurse, who immediately took the baby. He spent a bit more time with his wife and then went out of the room, seeing that she was falling asleep. Amelie did not hear the cannon fire, for the maid had closed the windows against the noise, but the prince had heard them from his study. He did count them, and there were indeed nineteen.

On that day, the young mother was also visited by the King and the Queen. Luis I and Maria Pia were truly happy. They had brought her presents, not lingering too long. They knew she was tired, as was to be expected. They congratulated her on the healthy and adorable child. Other close friends came to visit the Duchess, and then Carlos, the heir prince, returned.

6

"You didn't hear the cannons, did you?" he asked, smiling.

"No," his wife answered, "I fell asleep. Thank you for the ring. It is so beautiful! I will always wear it, just as I wear the ring from the birth of Prince Luis Felipe. Amelie had received a similar gift when the little girl was born, but she never wore that jewel, out of superstition. Who could tell?

"My parents, their Majesties, were here too," said Carlos. "They were so pleased that you are both in good health. Manuel will be Duke of Beja; we just need the King to sign the decree."

"Manuel will be happy, Carlos," Amelie told her husband. "He will never be king. The Duke of Beira, Luis Felipe, will be on the throne."

"Don't rush the future. My father is only 50, and my mother is just 41. They are young, and then I am also here, coming after them. They may still live for several more years," Carlos answered her.

"The longer, the better. From what I've understood, the situation is not exactly the best in our country. I don't want power on your shoulders, not just yet," Amelie whispered to him.

"What are you afraid of?"

"I'm not afraid; I probably feel this way because of Manuel's birth, but I shall soon recover. I can't wait to go out for a walk. I love Belem! It's a beautiful building with a lovely view. I like the banks of the river leading carefree beyond Lisbon. But now, I've become melancholic and I feel sleepy."

"Then, I let you sleep, and I'll see you tomorrow," said Carlos, kissing her softly. "Sweet dreams and sleep well! Leave your worries to me; I shall take care of everything."

After her husband left, Amelie thought about where her prince would go and with whom he would spend the evening, or even the night! The rumors that he had plenty of women had also reached her, but she didn't care. All the kings had the same behavior, not to mention an heir prince. She knew that she was safe. She had given him two boys, and she also knew that the love between them had turned into something powerful, indestructible. She had been taught from a young age; she knew about the possibility of such situations to occur, so her reactions were almost natural.

She would be the Queen. She knew it. She had the children as well as her husband's respect for her impeccable conduct, but she was especially young; she was 24, two years younger than her husband. It had been the right marriage, she thought, in between sleep and waking, eventually conquered by her desire to sleep long and well. She would see her child officially tomorrow, when Luis Felipe, the elder boy, would also come to meet his brother, who was two years younger; they were born two days apart in the same month. Luis Felipe had received, as a present for his birthday, a healthy little brother. Amelie fell asleep thinking that she and her husband were born on the same day, the 28th of September. That was a coincidence that greatly amused her, when she learned about it. She saw it as a divine sign. Amelie was already dreaming when the maid entered to draw the curtains. She was very careful not to wake up the future Queen, who was so tired then.

In the morning, Amelie felt better, but she was not allowed to get out of the bed. She was looking forward to seeing her children. When little Luis Felipe entered the room, he ran from the nurse to his mother's arms. She kissed him delightedly and asked if he wanted to see his younger brother. Luis Felipe answered without hesitating, in his own babbling language that he wanted to.

When the nurse brought the baby, the little prince received him with joy, for the baby was so small, and he was already so big. He asked many questions, and showed his feelings. As at a sign, Manuel also lifted a hand in is sleep. His brother caught it and wouldn't let it go.

"Mother, he is so small! I have to protect him when I grow up!" Luis Felipe said, full of the importance of his two years. "Look, he won't turn loose of my hand. He's asking me to look after him!"

Amelie told him that they must love each other when they grew up and that it was not a bad thing that he wanted to defend his little brother. Eventually, the baby let go of his brother's hand, yawning. Luis Felipe withdrew a bit and then climbed onto his mother's bed, under the governess's disapproving looks. But Amelie agreed to comply with the cold and strict rules only in public. When she was with her son, she forgot that he had to be raised to reign, but when she did think of that, she was glad that he was still young and that he belonged only to her.

She knew that in a couple of years her elder son would have to fulfill his duties, and would be his mother's boy for too short a time.

"At least I will have Manuel. He won't be raised in a strict manner; he belongs to me," she comforted herself in her mind. And then she still hoped she would have more children. From the depths of her heart, she wanted a little girl, who would also live. She prayed to Virgin Mary with her whole heart to spare her what had occurred the previous year. Everybody had been by her side, comforting her, as she recalled, but the wound in her heart was still raw, ready to open up again. Nobody knew how frightened she was for that birth and what bliss the doctors' pronouncement meant to her: Manuel was a healthy newborn baby. They would give him several names, as was the custom, but she wasn't at all interested in all those details.

Day after day, mother and son grew healthier and more vigorous. The morning when they were finally allowed to go out into the fresh air, what a glorious morning that was! Amelie was holding her baby as the nurse watched, idle.

"Manuel, my sweet baby, you are all mine ! Your brother will reign. Soon he will start to get a special education, but you will stay away from all these ugly things. You will truly enjoy a carefree life behind the throne. Your grandparents are young, so we can relax for the next several years."

The mother spoke to her child as if he were an adult. For certain, she loved both boys, but fate separated them, for one had to be the King, and the other would remain only the Duke of Beja, and thus closer to his mother.

Luis Felipe, who didn't understand much, heard every single day that he would eventually become the King, and he would rule. Amelie was tired of all those pointless discussions for a child who was only two years old. "And some country he will rule over, God!" she thought, with her lips tight.

Industrialization had brought about difficulties; political factions could not reach any compromise, and it seemed as if everything was going down into the ocean. There was a state of calm, of slack time, the calm before a terrible storm. A calm still possible to control, but she, like Queen Maria Pia, had never interfered in politics. Nonetheless, she had eyes to see and a lively soul to feel everything.

The christening of little Manuel was magnificent. There were so many guests who had come to congratulate them on their new baby, too many to count. They would not forget for a long time the banquet after the christening. Everybody had uncertainties in his/her own country, but that celebration made them all relax, and the ladies were exquisite, adorned with the jewels they took out of their jewel boxes only for special events like that one. Amelie looked so lovely. She was young and beautiful, and her three pregnancies had not changed her slim figure. Her husband also looked very handsome in his uniform. Even the king was lively. At midnight, the fireworks shook the windows of the royal residence, and the applause, shouting, and laughter lasted late into the evening. Children had not been awakened by the noises; they slept like angels, each one in his own bed.

Later, when everybody had left, Amelie went to see her children, her adored successors. Luis Felipe always slept uncovered, no matter how much his nanny strove to cover him. His young mother leaned over and kissed the bottom of his small, pink foot, then covered him, taking a finger to her lips, as a sign of silence to the nanny, who stood watching. Then Amelie went to the other room, where Manuel, with his small, tight fists, was happily sleeping, smiling at the angels in his dreams. Peacefully, she returned to her apartment. Carlos was not there, so she decided to get undressed and go to sleep without waiting for him.

She had decided a long time ago not to concern herself with her husband's escapades. She was happy with her motherhood, and with her inconspicuous presence, which she had chosen. After the maid left the room, Amelie lay down between the cold bed sheets and listened to the silence of night; the fresh air soothed her, especially after such a warm and tiring day. At last she fell asleep peacefully, and she woke up only in the morning.

Heat had gradually encompassed Lisbon. Under the trees in the palace park, the atmosphere was still, lacking any fresh breeze. In fact, no breeze made any leaf quiver. They had decided to go to Vila Vicosa to get away from the hot streets of the capital. They planned to leave a few days later. The children were both in good health, and Luis Felipe was growing taller and fonder of his brother.

Amelie was glad that her boys were close in age; two years meant almost nothing. The heir prince was caressing Manuel with a flower, which the baby was trying to catch. He was excitedly moving his legs, but couldn't reach it, then Luis was hiding it from his plump and greedy little hands and started laughing; their mother raised her eyes from the book she was reading, smiling to herself. Even the nannies were relaxed; one could seldom have seen children so kind, and so obedient, as they would sometimes say it.

Sometimes, those scenes were observed from one of the windows by Carlos, who would rarely go down to the park with his family. He loved Amelie and the boys with all his heart. But he had so much to do, to organize, so many solemn meetings he had to attend. His wife had little to do, she didn't get too much involved, but she also had a motivation for that: their newborn baby.

But they would go to Vila Vicosa together, just like on holiday, and almost like an ordinary family. The King and Queen would manage, as always, during the months of the second season of the year. There would be just the four of them, and they would all come back refreshed and renewed.

10

The stay during the whole summer in the royal residence of Vila Vicosa was, as they had hoped, peaceful and joyful. Manuel was growing and was already able to sit propped at his back, looking at the people and not just lying down. How astonished he was when he realized that difference! Sometimes Carlos would go to the capital when his most urgent duties required that, but he would come back to start all over, to re-enter the fairytale-like atmosphere, which would be the last one lived with no care.

That is how the summer months passed, as Amelie bloomed all over again, and the children grew more and more attached to each other. The boys liked to throw a ball to each other, a soft, small rubber ball. You should have heard the yelling when Manuel failed to catch it. It was as if a terrible thing had happened, but then he would take it back from his mother and throw it all over again, just as clumsily, to his brother, who laughed happily. In the evening at bedtime, they were so tired that they fell asleep immediately. During their holidays, they would smell like earth, flowers, and liberty. And then September came, and they all had to leave the palace for the dusty and increasingly dangerous Lisbon.

They freshened the atmosphere at the palace when they returned all rested – full of the rest that was so far from the Court. The King and Queen were delighted to see their grandchildren. It seemed to Amelie, though, that her father-in-law was a bit pale, and she asked Carlos what he thought about that.

"It's nothing, dear; he's just tired, and don't forget – he hasn't left on holidays. Maybe he will feel better now that the children are here, for he loves them, and they will cheer him up. While we were away, my brother did not quite know how to replace us. The Duke of Porto is often absent. He has his activities that we don't know about."

"Maybe he envies you for being the firstborn child," Amelie told him.

"Who, Afonso? Never. You know he is rather strange, and he has not been raised to be a king. He had a freer education, just as Manuel will have. In four years, Luis Felipe will start such an instruction, but not his brother," Carlos continued.

"I wish the king would live long, so that we would be able to still avoid those responsibilities," Amelie said.

"You will become the Queen anyway," Carlos told her, taking her by the shoulders and turning her toward him. "Just as Luis Felipe will be King when I am no longer alive. The King, my father, is young. He may still be there on the throne for quite some time. But I do not wish to talk about this subject. I would prefer not to take the throne so soon, either."

"He didn't have that pallour when we left to Vila Vicosa. This is the first time I have noticed that about the good king," Amelie repeated sadly.

The discussion ended there. Nobody could control anybody else's destiny, and anyway, it would be impossible to be able to influence another's fortune. Fate is embedded in one's being; the ball of life is unique and belongs exclusively to its owner. That's why Luis I's sudden death, in late October, took everyone by surprise except for Amelie.

King Luis I, as a child, was not raised to reign; he had been like her Manuel. He was not the firstborn son of the family; he was the son of Maria II and Fernando II. He loved writing poetry; that was his means of relaxation. He also had another delight in his life: the ocean with all its unknown elements. He had spent a fortune on ships built especially to observe the sea creatures. He had come to the throne subsequent to his brother Pedro V's death, for the latter had no heirs. His succession to the throne was quite a surprise to him, a surprise that took him away from his poetry notebooks, but which did not make him give up the curiosities of the ocean.

The young and beautiful Queen Amelie recalled the visit to the huge Aquarium Vasco da Gama, where she had seen some animals she never imagined to exist. That huge Aquarium, open to the public, was established by King Luis I himself, "The Popular," as he was called.

There were so many clamoring in the street to view the coffin of the King, gone so soon, that it made one wonder how they could crowd any more people in Lisbon's streets. Who would have thought he would die so soon? Maria Pia, who had become then the Queen Mother, could not get over it. She was inconsolable. The one who had supported her all his life was no longer there to tap her slightly on her hand, calming her. For him, she had left her father's Italy; she had reigned with him so many full years. And he was only 42. He would first read his poems to her, before their marriage in 1862. He was a King, but he had always proved to be a romantic soul as well. She would now withdraw into herself and support her son, who had become King at such a young age.

Amelie, who was now the Queen, was amazed at how that year, 1889, had changed her life completely. She had wanted one thing, and something else would follow! In fact, she knew she was ready, but it had come too soon, and too painfully, I would say. Carlos even asked her how she had that premonition regarding his father, and Queen Amelie shrugged her shoulders and smiled a bit.

"I don't know," she said, tightly holding her husband's hand. "I just know that now we have some other duties, different ones, which we haven't had before, but we will manage to fulfill them. I shall support you!"

"Thank you," Carlos replied, kissing her on her forehead. He loved his wife very much, and his affairs with mistresses didn't matter. He knew to be generous with his mistresses, but his wife belonged to him alone. She was the one who gave him the boys who would take his name further. The Portuguese monarchy would not perish; he was convinced of that.

The young Queen and King received a host of congratulatory letters, but one pleased them especially. Carlos's best friend, Alberto I of Monaco, sent felicitations, and from the letter, one could sense his genuine joy and desire to have them visit him in his princedom as soon as possible. The young monarchs thus started a round of visits in Spain, France, and the United Kingdom, ending with their visit with Alberto who shared the same passion for the sea that Carlos had inherited from his father Luis I.

Amelie could hardly wait to go back home. She missed her children and her adopted country, as well as her beautiful and favorite Belem. When they reached Lisbon, she felt such a relief, being a genuinely happy hostess for the Kingdom's guests. During that time, they had been visited by the King of Spain, the King of the United Kingdom, by the German Guillerme II, and also by the French President, Emile Loubet.

Everything had begun auspiciously, but gradually it all started to change. Carlos displayed his mistresses in full view of the public, and he was extravagant and extremely prodigal with those ladies. Amelie dedicated herself to their two children, supported by the Queen Mother, who encouraged her, soothing her, and convincing her not to make a scene. What would have been the point?

The political situation in the country, just as throughout Europe, was disastrous. It was obvious that in Europe, Portugal had little influence, especially after it assigned its colonies to Great Britain by two treaties that infuriated the Portuguese. They had not assigned all of them, but most of them, and nobody offered assistance through diplomacy channels to help them regain those colonies from the British. Without the major resources that were given to the English, Portugal experienced two total bankruptcies, which highly inflamed the political class, when two other factions came upon the stage: the Republicans and the Socialists. The newspapers raged against Carlos I and the monarchy. Instigators were everywhere, shouting invectives against the king. They demanded that all men, not just the educated and wealthy ones, have the right to vote.

Under those circumstances, Joao Franco was appointed Prime Minister, and with the consent and support of the King, he began a dictatorship. The presence of the two Queens, the King's brother, and heir to the throne, Luis Felipe notwithstanding, no change occurred. The dictatorship continued and increasing hatred against the monarchy reached a dizzying level. In these years, politically summarized, the two children were educated differently. In the early years they were left together, and they came to understand each other perfectly. They helped each other, they played with each other, they would run after various things in the park, imagining themselves as pirates or all sorts of other wonderful characters from stories. At one point, however, Luis Felipe began his education to become king, and reluctantly the two children spent less time together.

"I will be king; you will not," Luis said to Manuel at one point. "You'll play, you'll learn something else, but I am bound to the throne."

Manuel did not reply; he was like the child who lets the bird in his hand fly away. He had other children to play with, but he longed for his older brother – in vain, however. He was guided toward literature, while the one who would become King was directed toward politics and political studies. Manuel was not jealous. He liked to read, to study Portuguese literature and the history of the country of his birth. He could speak French, and he enjoyed music so much that he was provided with a good piano teacher. He learned to ride and play tennis, which his older brother did not have in his educational program. Luis Felipe, to relax, had to choose among physical exercises of various kinds.

Manuel was happy. He enjoyed a warm relationship with all the children of the court, and he was allowed to play and do many things that his brother was not allowed. He had many teachers who implanted in his mind great knowledge of mathematics, French, English, Latin, and German, making young Duke of Beja a pleasant young man of many interests.

For the first time, the young man made a trip abroad in 1903 with his mother and the Crown Prince, where he amazed everyone with his vast knowledge. Egypt seemed colossal and he was especially fascinated by the pharaohs, extraordinarily endowed men who left behind so many amazing pieces. He loved new things and was not interested at all in the financial crisis and the bankruptcy of the country. He had been raised otherwise,

14

while Luis Felipe was anxious to return to the country and use his resources to save his country and of course his monarchical future.

The next year, completely unexpectedly, the Queen and King became parents for the fourth time. Finally, they had a girl, whom they baptized Maria Melchora. Manuel was very happy, for she looked like his mother, whom he idolized. He was fifteen when that little girl was born in 1904, and Luis Felipe was seventeen. For the first heir, the joy was smaller, for he had to reign soon, so he could not think very seriously about his little sister. The most enchanted were Queen Amelie and young Manuel. To the Queen Mother, that birth was something incomprehensible – that child conceived by the queen at age 39.

In fact, Luis Felipe de Braganza was preparing his entry into the world next to his father. They had both gone abroad with the trip ending in something unheard of at the time, the visit of the Crown Prince to the colonies that the Portuguese Crown still owned. No one had ever heard about such a venture, and nothing like that had ever been done since Joao VI. They had been the center of attention throughout Europe, and Luis was very proud. So there were some good things about being the Crown Prince, and he had his moments of pleasure and entertainment, which flattered his vanity somewhat.

While Luis Felipe was praised for his visit with the King in the colonies, Manuel was close to his mother and his three-year old sister, thinking very seriously about a career in the naval field. He was not afraid of death threats that Republicans threw around. He knew that those actions were real; he knew that his brother travelled armed, but he did not give so much importance to those things. He was a dreamer after all. He always said he was not natured to be a king, for he was too great a dreamer, not like Luis Felipe who took his role seriously.

When his older brother met him in the garden, he would briefly burst out and tell him up pointedly that he did not understand what Manuel found so wonderful about the planting of small roots with two leaves on top that he enjoyed so much."I find life, Luis Felipe! These plants will grow, bloom, and spread seeds for the future!"

In response to his brother, the Crown Prince shrugged and left. "I love him, he is my brother, but he is too different from me. He was allowed to behave differently and had a different education." Manuel knew he was loved, too, but a future king was aware that he could not plant seedlings. Or could he?

The year of 1907 was full of riots, the pent-up exasperation from those who no longer wanted King Carlos. They had had enough of his lifestyle. The two political groups, the Republicans and the Socialists, were showing their teeth more and more often against the monarchy. The royal family decided to spend the holidays and the first month of the New Year in the palace of the Dukes of Braganza , their official haven at Vila Vicosa. They needed a rest and more coherent, rational thinking. Death threats were becoming more frequent against King Carlos I.

They left before Christmas when they felt cheerful, their hearts loaded with courage and love. Amelie, however, went with a twist of anxiety, which she explained to herself when they arrived at the residence. She had forgotten the ring her husband gave her upon the birth of the heir. She was not superstitious by nature, but still something clutched at her chest when she thought about it. It was a small matter; she would find it when they returned to Lisbon.

The Queen had left her mark, her "imprint" on the palace forever, for she had brought many improvements over several years. Everyone loved that Alentejo area. The building was surrounded by olive groves and plenty of water – a miracle considering the hot climate of Portugal. In front of the palace there was the Augustinian Church, where the Queen loved to go alone, because there, no one dared to rail against them. In fact, this was the only place where the royal label was not so rigorous; none of the court was there, only a few close believers.

At one of the tables, Carlos even reminded those who were present, but especially his two sons that:

"These lands are those from which the Dukes of Braganza have drawn their life strength and vitality, to rise up and follow their destiny for centuries. It is a blessed land, where we are untouchable. Here no one will dare attack us or spread dirt about us in the newspapers. Alentejo is royalist, proud that we come from its orchards and clear waters.

Amelie looked silently at her three men. She had been to church in the morning and shared her fears with her beloved priest who respected her and always encouraged her.

"Your fears, my daughter, are justified, but the Lord is aware and will watch over your family. Marvelous things are happening all over Europe; the wave is everywhere, not just in our country," he told her quietly, touching her gently.

The Queen startled slightly when she heard the applause after her husband gave the toast. She barely heard a thing and mechanically took the champagne glass to her mouth. She wanted to go for a walk, and when they finished eating, she went out and sat on a bench in the lovely orchard, which gave the impression of safety, of a wall. She thought she was alone, but a rustle made her stand up. It was Manuel, her younger son.

"MomMother, what are you doing here alone?" he asked, surprised.

"I am in a state of confusion that I cannot explain," she replied.

"Perhaps you are thinking about the King and my brother. I read the manifestos and the Republican newspapers, even if I was forbidden to. If you read them, you will see only hatred and too much blood everywhere. I know you will not tell anyone that I have read this. I immediately threw the papers into the fire, so there's no sign of disobedience on my part," Manuel said, smiling at his mother.

"Yes, they think, Manuel. I'm afraid! And the fear hurts more than my inability to do something. I do not like fear, but I live with it, and I cannot dismiss it like something ordinary."

"Mother, this proves that even royalty have feelings just like any ordinary people, that we are fearful; we are afraid, and we also think about tomorrow. Republicans say bad things about my father, claiming that he is extravagant and careless and spends a lot of money on his mistresses."

"Hush, son, do not remind me! I was raised to cope with this kind of thing. The King is my husband and the father of my children, nothing else, and then, all Kings are the same. He is not the only one with these unfortunate habits. I forgave him a long time. It's a closed topic."

"Forgive me, Mother! I did not want to open this subject. That is what I read."

"You need to see your father, the King, as the perfect man, the best man, so do not bend your ear to what the world says about him."

"This is precisely how I see him, Mother, just as you said, and also I see my brother as monarch. But I want to tell you that I'm happy with my life. I never wanted to be King; I do not think I would like that. I am much more a dreamer, an idealist. But here they come," Manuel said, pointing to the end of the alley.

Father and son, King and Crown Prince, approached the bank on which the two were sitting.

"There you are! You left so quickly from the table," Carlos said.

"My head ached, my husband, and here it is so peaceful. Manuel showed up from nowhere, and we remained here."

"Yes, it is the only peaceful place right now," the King said with a sigh. "We are going to the end of the orchard, near the water. Will you come?"

"No, dear," said the Queen, "we will stay here; you go your way."

17

The King said goodbye, Luis Felipe smiled, and then they moved along.

"There they go," murmured the queen. "How strange! I have rarely seen them like this!"

"What did you say, Mother?" Manuel asked, sitting down on the bench again.

"Nothing, dear. I was talking to myself, my thoughts," his mother answered, holding the shawl tighter. "I think it would be better to go back. I wonder what the Queen Mother and my sweet little girl are doing."

"I think they are both sleeping. Vila Vicosa is restful. We always sleep so soundly here. I think I will sleep like a baby tonight."

"I hope so, my son; I cannot rest anywhere anymore; I feel something, but I do not know what. I went to Father Eugenio, but this time he didn't manage to reassure me, either. He saw the fear in my eyes and saw that I left him as troubled as I came. I think I grieved the holy old man. He has always loved me. I think it is sad that he could not give me courage."

"Come, Mother, do not think about it. When you see Maria, you will forget everything; you so wanted a little girl." Manuel offered his arm to his mother and they walked toward the palace, the opposite direction from where the King and Luis Felipe went. It was as if they had separated their destinies.

Christmas came full of gifts, and everyone was joyful and relaxed. The attraction was the Infanta, who was beginning to understand things around her at her delightful age of three years. Maria Pia, Queen Mother, went off to bed, her body asking for rest. Infanta fell asleep, too, among the gifts and did not wake up when the nurse took her in her arms.

"She will sleep in the clothes she is wearing right now," her mother smiled, kissing her blonde curls.

They sat for a while, played some cards, laughed at one another when they lost, and thus Christmas passed, happy days full of family warmth. Few were the moments when they had enjoyed something like that. For the first time, Amelie fell fast asleep and dreamed until morning. The dream showed her with her two sons and the King in a green field full of poppies, like blood in the field. They were walking and running; they even seemed to have a ball which they threw at each other, laughing and happy with the joy of the game. Suddenly Manuel threw the ball a little too hard, not toward his playmate, but toward his father. Carlos ran after the

18

ball, and the ball magically ran as well, farther and farther, until the King vanished from sight.

"See what you did?" Luis Felipe shouted at his brother who remained where he was. "You ruined the game!"

The Prince ran after his father to help him stop the ball, but he also disappeared. The two who remained there waited for a while and then began to look for them, to call them, but there was no sign of the King or the Prince.

Amelie woke up terrified. "Both of them!" she whispered. "Manuel will be king! He went after the ball. God! This is what my anxiety means!" She closed that dream deep down in her heart and placed her head back on the pillows. It was not yet time to wake up.

The New Year celebrations passed when the cannons fired at midnight, joining with all the church bells. They raised a glass of champagne and wished each other a happy New Year 1908, truly happy and safe for all. They would stay one more month; Carlos had decided that the prime minister could do without him or if necessary, contact him at the Vila Vicosa for critical issues. Franco was seen coming and going just as discreetly. He did not want to disturb the royal family vacation. He sometimes had a disconcerted, altered look, but the reasons for this seriousness were not overtly disclosed by him or the King.

Everyone knew that they wanted to remove the King. He had a great many guards now. But anti-monarchist groups were also more vigilant. Perhaps the King suspected that there was a traitor in his entourage, but did not mention this to his family. He knew to appear dignified and unafraid in the face of destiny. And then there was another month's holiday in beautiful Vila Vicosa, which he would devote to his family; it would be wonderful to forget his political troubles.

January was a pleasant month with no rain or very little. The weather was not so hot, and one could walk freely among the olive trees. Even Luis Felipe rediscovered his cheerfulness and his brother at the same time. He forgot for a while that he was Crown Prince and joined his brother in his various pleasant activities.

"You know, Manuel, that your life is more beautiful and peaceful than mine. You can afford to be at ease, as you wish; you will always be a free man. You won't be forced to attend state protocols, boring visits next to two-faced people. There are always people of that kind at our father. I have had the opportunity to see and realize that. Few people really love him and are faithful to him. Times are changing…."

"We love him a lot, Luis! And he knows that, but he has a destiny to fulfill, as do you. And I have a destiny, which is to sit in the shade and support you from behind, minding my own business," Manuel said after a moment. "I love gardening; it always calms me. I like to water my flowers, and you see that here they have taken over the garden. It is beautiful, but we could do more if there was enough money."

Luis smiled at his brother, continuing his walk in the nicely drawn paths of the city. Sunday they all went to church, where they remained until the end of the Mass. They always waited for the priest's blessing. That old almost spartan church inspired them with its durability and reminded them of what the House of Braganza meant for the people.

There were also citizens of the city on these occasions, the common people, who loved their king. They thought a monarchy was the way governance should be, and they did not understand the desire of some for change. They went about their daily life and faith. For them, Braganza palace was a royalist symbol; a new era, one that had no precedent in history, was inconceivable to them. Novelty caused anxiety to them. They were proud when they saw the whole royal family in prayer. For that time, it felt as if they were all equal before God and His Church. And the royal family loved watching their subjects together with them in the church. Their modesty always impressed the royals, and it was as if for a few moments, life became simpler.

Only the Queen Mother did not see any of this. Since she had withdrawn, she had built a world of her own and was always speaking about the Italy of her heart. If she had been able to, she would have gone back to her ancestors; in her mind, I think she was already doing that. She had started to love her little granddaughter also because she was so young and not yet tight-laced in court etiquette. So Infanta Maria always had a personal ally. She liked for her grandmother to show her old pictures, notebooks filled with drawings, her collection of photographs. Infanta never ruined or destroyed what the Queen Mother gave her; on the contrary, she was very responsible for her age. Maria Pia always said that she took after the late king, which enchanted the little girl, who would immediately point to him in a picture. Being born so late, she was the family toy and jewel. Everyone wanted her to themselves, even for a moment, but she preferred her grandmother and her mother. Manuel sometimes would get the chance to play with her, but the others didn't really have that privilege, for she would immediately run away, because they were too serious for her.

It had been just a dream, that January of 1908. It felt as if the family had become closer, which strengthened them. Franco insistently begged the King to return, however, so Carlos, under duress, set the date at last: February 1, 1908. They had a few days left before that, so they could still be at ease. Everyone seemed rejuvenated, with the energy to move forward. When preparations for the departure were ready, they set off to Lisbon in full view of the ordinary, good, and faithful people in Vila Vicosa.

CHAPTER 3

Carlos, the King, was a bit apprehensive. Franco often brought to his attention that the joke with the revolutions was getting serious, asking in what country do people go out in the streets and claim their rights. He told him about the increasingly harsh strikes in factories, all destabilizing the leadership of the countries. He reminded Carlos one more time about the disastrous situation in their own country, since the end of the Old World. There were all kinds of clandestine groups established solely with a view to removing the royalty and proclaiming the Republic as everyone's hope for the future, dazzling them and making them dream. Carlos kept this warning to himself, thinking that there were two sons behind him if something happened to him. The Queen was noticed all of that, but she kept silent, trying to appear as normal as possible. She couldn't do much anyway. Vacation was over, and they had to face everything once they arrived in the capital.

They were traveling in a spacious car in which the whole family would fit, to Berreiro, where they would embark upon a ship that would take them quietly down the Tejo to Lisbon. The weather was lovely and the landscape was beautiful along the placid waterway. On both banks of the magnificent river, willow branches bent to touch the small waves continuously dancing. Birds startled by the noise would shriek and dart off into the blue sky of that day. The little girl would point at them and laugh with delight when they became flustered and dashed from their perch. A bit later, Infanta fell asleep, tired from the fresh air. The nanny took her in her arms, and that was all the baby waited for. She felt warm and content.

The king was watching, smiling at that intimate family portrait. The guard watching over him was on the alert, and he felt safe. He looked forward to returning and putting the reins on the leadership of his kingdom, which he wished were stronger, from a political and financial point of view. He looked at his wife, but she was watching the water leading to her to Belem, to her dear home, to which she had become completely attached. There, all her children had been born; there, she would withdraw when she wanted to be alone. And she wanted to arrive faster and get some rest. It was as if the realization that the vacation was over had completely exhausted her. The respite had been wonderful, with so few people around, just the family and a few close friends. The guards had not been so strict either.

Soon, they would be in the center of Lisbon; there, in Cais do Sodre they would go ashore and take an open carriage to the Royal Palace. When the company set off, surrounded by the guards, Lisbon was teeming with activity, which was quite ordinary to the King. Usually, there would be a lot of people waving and throwing flowers to the king. The Queen was given an exquisite bouquet of flowers, which she brought to her face, drawing in the heavenly fragrance. Imperceptibly, the carriage turned toward the Terreiro do Paco street. Manuel was thinking that he would have to resume his studies at the Naval Academy. Soon, he would have a serious activity to accomplish.

There were multitudes of people there. The King was smiling, glad to be reaching their home soon. They were tired and ready for a cup of tea, which they all deserved. They had barely gotten to the street when several short gunshots destroyed everyone's dream. Screams could be heard, and then people starting pushing and shoving.

The inhabitants of the city were witnessing a political and simultaneously, a family drama. Their King, Carlos I, had been shot to death, and his heir was dying. The two Republican fanatics were caught and killed. Franco, who was also in the entourage when the King came down from the boat, was shouting orders, extremely agitated and yet articulate.

"Save the heir prince, Luis Felipe!" he shouted feverishly.

Somebody took Manuel, who was only injured, to look after him. The women escaped. Those two assassins had aimed so well! Nobody was imagining any longer; now everybody understood that Portugal was going through a metamorphosis. It was turning into blood. The Queen Mother was screaming, driven mad, for her son, traumatized by what she had lived and was still living. Queen Amelie was striking at the corners of the carriage with the flowers she had kept. Luis was mortally wounded, almost unconscious as death closed in, clearly written on his face. He smiled with his last strength, supported by the doctors' hands.

"Manuel," he said slowly to his brother standing next to him, "even a gardener can be a king!"

The Duke of Beja kept silent as the doctors removed the bullets from his arm. He only sighed as he watched his brother, who was looking at him, almost dead. He knew when Luis breathed his last, and he became frightened. The Queens started screaming when the heir prince left this world to join his father. It seemed that in their anguish they had forgotten about Manuel. When one of the doctors told them he was out of danger and that he would live, they rushed to him like birds of prey. They realized that the monarchy would go on through this son whom no one had ever thought would be King. But Manuel was tired, exhausted by the extraction of the bullets, and saw as if through fog the two bodies next to each other, both gone to eternity.

Maria Pia, the Mother Queen, lost her mind when she saw the two bleeding bodies one next to the other, father and son. She could not grasp such horror. She had fallen from the precipice of eternal grief. The Prime Minister gave the necessary dispositions for the national funerals. He was deeply shaken by what those insane men had done. Those two, shot after the attack, were identified as members of the radical group Carbonaria. But it didn't matter anymore that their names were Alfredo Costa and Manuel Buica. Franco was simply afraid of the consequences of a monarchy with a king who had not been raised toward that position, young and lacking any political knowledge. His very career was at stake, his dictatorship was falling down subsequent to these two unfortunate and untimely deaths.

Queen Amelie was not thinking of that. She knew she would support her son until the very end, until her last drop of blood. She knew he was an innocent, prey in the mouth of wolves, but that he simply had to carry on the House of Braganza and the monarchy. She trusted the doctors; Manuel was young and would survive. There were also the two funerals, and she could not rest before her son recovered and was proclaimed King. He must not risk his life, especially since the Republicans failed eventually. That boy was alive to carry on the monarchy in Portugal. But for how long? "Time will tell," Amelie thought, sighing painfully.

Eventually they left to go to the Belem palace. It was with difficulty that the Queen Mother was taken away from her son, but it was necessary to put the two of them into coffins, after a thorough washing, and then take them to Palacio de Necesidades, the King's Palace. The mind of Queen Maria Pia was thoroughly shaken. She would not recover from the shock for the rest of her life. They made it safely to the palace, where Manuel went to his room after everybody was assured that all was well.

He lay down on his bed, and started to unbutton his tunic, which was destroyed at the arm. He sighed with sorrow and lay down. First dizziness seized him, to which was added fatigue and the shock of the day which had changed his destiny. He saw his mother with her hair completely dishevelled, shouting and beating the flowers against the figure at the carriage corners, a desperate figure to whom nothing happened, but who saw it all. So what if the killers were killed? That didn't matter anymore. He fell asleep at last, and did not waken when his mother came to see what he was doing. Amelie was distressed watching the servants put black cloth at all the balconies. That was a color she had always hated.

The Queen Mother had fallen asleep after the doctors gave her some powders to help her rest, but Amelie refused to sleep. She wanted to be witness to history. She knew that that violence would not bring about any peace and that nothing would be right in Manuel's reign. Sometimes she thought about letting go of everything and going away. Life was important. She saw clearly that one could be a king in one moment, and just moments later, one could be history.

She remained in the salon, apathetic, leaning her head on her hands. Through a fog, she saw the Prime Minister coming in, saw him bow.

"Your Majesty," he said, "the bodies of the king and of the prince are prepared to go to Palacio de Necesidades. I ordered many flowers and I arranged the large room. Everybody will be able to pay a last tribute to them."

"You see, Sir," the queen slowly spoke, "kings are humans too; when fate is to be met, no guard, no matter how large, can do much. One single bullet, or two, in the case of Portugal, and everybody goes away. I no longer believe in a monarchy in this country full of hatred. I shall undoubtedly support my son, but I shall not risk his life. May God's will be done! If he must abdicate, I shall accept that for the sake of my family's life and future. I have seen too much today, which has changed my views." Amelie stood up and went to the window, pointing to the shrouds. "Everything is black. I dislike these windows," she said. "I know why you came. Manuel has to be proclaimed King immediately. Do you think I can wake him up? I can't. I've been in his apartment and I saw him sleeping. I don't even know what kind of king he will be, after all, for he likes fencing, horseback riding, working in the garden. He plays the piano beautifully and he is passionate about plants."

"This is what I wanted to talk to you about," said Franco, bowing. "But we can wait until tomorrow. The papers are ready, we just need a signature. As for his disposition toward beautiful things, I think he will have to forget about them soon."

"My God," the queen replied, "aren't you afraid?"

"Yes, I am. I shall fall simultaneously with this child who will become the King, but I undertake this destructive gesture. Somebody else will take my place; Manuel, the young prince, is a peaceful romantic. I don't think he will be as firm in his position as his father. Now, if you will please allow me to go, I shall take care of everything, and I shall be ahead of the convoy to the Kings' Palace. I can see and fully understand that I shall be alone. I do hope I will come out of this trip alive. Tomorrow you will have to be seen there, too."

"We shall all be there," said Amelie, "and Manuel will sign that paper, becoming the King. But for today, this is enough."

The Prime Minister took a bow and left to make sure the procession would be done in perfect order. The cavalry was much more numerous, and the rows of guards were also reinforced. The next day, Portugal would have a new King!

The next morning, Manuel signed the papers and thus was proclaimed King of Portugal. There was little joy. Congratulations were diminished by the force of the events that occurred the previous day. The young King, with his bandaged arm, accompanied his family to the palace where his father and brother were surrounded by flowers, crowns, flags, and especially that hideous black cloth, Amelie's obsession those days.

The people greeted the new King, who was barely eighteen, and he learned to put on smiles and wave his healthy hand in greeting. In his heart, he wished he could be anywhere else but there, but he had no choice. In a way, he had now become serene. Maria Pia, the Queen Mother, was peaceful thanks only to the medicines. She would become hysterical when she remembered and when the pain started to bite, piercing her heart.

Those days passed, and the two were laid to rest in the Royal Pantheon of the House of Braganza, next to their ancestors, more or less fortunate. The Sao Vicente da Fora Church was full of guests, and the streets around it hummed with people. The ordinary, simple Portuguese people had grown fond of that young and unfortunate King, acclaiming him from their hearts. Manuel could feel their affection, and he seemed to forget about his grief, wishing to serve all his Portuguese subjects. He was no longer a boy then; he was a King. He didn't know why his thoughts had taken him to Egypt and a different king, almost a child, but he immediately forgot about it, looking forward to ruling his country.

26

CHAPTER 4

His country, which in a few days, had forgotten about the murder of the two kings, was now trying to speculate somehow upon the naiveté and the inexperience of this young King, too young and too educated in everything except the job of king. His good fortune was his mother, Amelie, who guided him from her heart as she had promised a few days before. The Queen Mother had the support of the great politician Jose Luciano do Castro, who was trying as best he could, through advice, to mitigate the King's youth.

After the discussions that this trio had, Manuel realized that the leadership style adopted by his father had led to the disastrous consequences in 1908. Coming to understand only too well the state of affairs in the country at that particular time, he decided that he would rule the country, but he would not govern – in other words, he would get involved less in the State matters.

One of his first deeds as monarch was to demand the resignation of Dictator Joao Franco and his cabinet, a demand that the Prime Minister was expecting, too, and to which he agreed with no hesitation. He knew, and he realized that Manuel did not have much choice. The boat was already adrift in the middle of the ocean with no possibility to ask for anyone's help. The monarchy was perishing with every single day that passed. They held free elections, much desired by the political parties. The Republicans and the rest of the opposition received only 42% of the votes, and the monarchic parties got the majority. But what was the use? Manuel was helpless. He did not know how to manage that advantage because of his lack of experience, and although he was a beloved King, he did not succeed in bringing to his dynasty house, the House of Braganza, its former prestige.

After those elections, there was formed a government of national union, led by Francisco Joaquin Ferreira da Amaral. What did the young King feel on the 6th of May, 1908? That is not hard to guess. Not joy, at any rate, even if the two queens were smiling warmly at him from the balcony. That was the day of his coronation, when he swore he would be faithful to the Constitution of his beloved Portugal, even if he felt the clouds gathering above his head.

The King thought that a reign begun under the auspices of blood is not of good omen, but thankfully, he was not a superstitious young man. One couldn't possibly be superstitious when he is eighteen and the wind of youth driving powerfully the ship of enthusiasm and optimism. He had gotten that idea in his head and he knew he was not wrong. He was waiting for something to happen, something that would unchain him, make him feel free. He could feel it in his bones, see it in the eyes of the Republicans. He was calmly watching those assassins of his father. What could he do? He had been forced to sustain a new form of governance for the prestige and reinforcement of his royal house. He did what he had to do, but when he was alone in Palacio de Necesidades, he knew that he was not reinforcing any prestige.

He was prepared for anything; he felt no more pain. That pain had been buried with his father and Luis Felipe. Sometimes he thought of his brother. Luis would have known how to rule. He had been trained for that. He was twenty, two years older than Manuel, at the time of the murder.

The new King began a long tour in his country, where he found much sympathy and adoration from simple people who truly loved him.

"What's the use," he thought "when these people who love me probably have never been to the capital, and have no idea what the poisonous fangs of power are like!" His first visit was to Porto, and during his chain of visits, he inaugurated a new railway in Espinho. They all received him well, in every Lusitanian corner his boots stepped into. The sympathy toward the child-king grew continuously because ordinary men and women perceived him only through his youth and beauty. They did not see behind his back the political dirt by which he was inevitably touched.

Manuel, the young King, made courtesy visits outside his country, where he was also well received, with much condescension, by each of the State heads. In Paris, he even fell in love for the first time – for a starlet, a beautiful young actress, unexpectedly discreet for such a woman. She was his only mistress during his bachelorhood. The affair of Manuel and Gaby Deslys was handled quietly and tastefully, with the actress entering and leaving Portugal unannounced without anyone knowing her identity. When she was "caught" and assailed by journalists, Gaby gave no information; she only smiled and replied "Who, me? The King's lover? Hmm ...." Her discretion greatly increased her esteem in the eyes of the young King, who saw her as a refuge for his ill-fated, difficult days. She fully deserved all the gifts that Manuel gave her. Even after the deposition in 1910, they met again when she was in London, but one year later, she decided to go and pursue her career in the United States, and their love cooled. Manuel shrugged, understood and accepted the destiny that Divinity gave him. Soon he forgot her, too, for there was no other choice.

That relationship, as I have previously stated, was the only one the King had. And it was not a daily relationship; Manuel and Gaby saw each other only when the King would to go Paris or when Gaby would come to Lisbon. Therefore, one should not pay too much attention to their relationship. Young Manuel had too much on his mind back then.

Normally, Portugal is mostly an agrarian country, with surprisingly little industry for the early 20th century. The European uprisings should have touched it less. Those troubled moments on the continent provided the fortuitous pretext for the Republicans to create disagreements among those governing. Manuel had to support the Socialists, who were more moderate in their actions. He asked them to re-organize the country on a realistic basis, according to its peculiarities.

The King, fully supported by his mother, took frequent trips, but he tried to have especially close relations, as close as possible, with the country Amelie had been born in. It is known that the British have always been allies of the Portuguese. So hopes were focused on the Island. A marriage with an English princess seemed ideal with a view toward reinforcing Portugal's ties and connections with England. But that wish did not come true, because of the British government's opposition, apprehensive since the events in 1908. That government realized the uncertainty of the country led by House of Braganza.

Manuel accepted that decision and tried to channel his efforts toward possibly restoring the country. He tried, with the help of some experts, to establish a National Institute of Labor in September of 1910, but that initiative came too late for the constitutional monarchy that had long been adrift.

The young twenty-year old king realized the precarious state of his ostensible reign. In a discussion with his mother, he presented his ideas, which Amelie listened to with full approval.

"Mother," he said, "in these two years, I've counted seven governments that have come and gone from the country's leadership, each with its own ideas which contradicted one another and destabilized the country even more. I read in the newspapers that the Republican party is rising in the polls, while the monarchic parties forget why they exist, grating on each other's nerves. I believe that this is the end of the monarchy, and we should prepare for the worst. We don't have internal support, not to mention any external one. All the countries face the same problems as we do. The Republican party will take action radically and with force, as they did in 1908. I no longer have any doubts about it and I am tired of sitting in between two political ideologies. It's never a good thing to be in the middle; I've learned that. Yes, the people love me, but they are naive and they mind their own life, as long as their interests are managed. The Republicans will take daring action, even if there are not many of them, but they have increased compared to what they were two years ago. Sooner or later, a month or a year from now, you will agree with me."

"You are seeing things too harshly, but what you say is true," Amelie told him. "You've grown up, my darling, in these years. Too bad you can't show what you can do with your brilliant mind. Luis Felipe leamt all that from the books, but you've learned it the hard way. If need be, we shall leave. I don't want to lose another son. I have discussed this with Castro. My family is far more important, and you see the condition your grandmother is in. She still has not been able to come to terms with what happened two years ago. I don't think she could bear another episode like that."

That discussion, which they had in September, proved to become fact only one month later. Lisbon had turned hostile during that recent time. Amelie went together with the Queen Mother to the family Pantheon, and privately said goodbye to all those who rested there. Kings from ancient times, infants with huge crinolines, the Queen talked to them all, while Maria Pia waited for her on a bench. The elder Queen was in a strange condition, and she had grown tired of walking around through so many mortuary stones. She remained in front of her son and that too-recent gravestone. They did not linger, but left quickly from there. They knew it was not a good thing to be obvious in any way.

Amelie had secretly written a letter with her seal to the United Kingdom asking for help and expressing her desire to return to the house where she had been born, if necessary. She received a brief and favorable answer. If need be, everything would be arranged and prepared. The Queen was relieved that no one had intercepted her letters; they still had those loyal to the crown, she thought. The King agreed with her, and just in case – a case he hoped would never occur – he had prepared a ship, its purpose and destination unknown to the Republicans. They had friends who had put their lives in jeopardy for the royal family. They were to remain, and if they were discovered, they would bear the consequences.

Early October found the King in his palace. He was closed in his study with a book in his hand. It was quiet in the palace, apparently more peaceful, but it had happened before that Manuel did not hear a thing around him. Since that ship had been prepared for his exile, he felt more confident. He knew that he would not die like his father, like a mouse in a trap. Just then, his faithful butler, the one who had carried him in his arms and watched him grow up, entered, telling Manuel the news.

"What is it, Angelo?"

"Your Majesty, one can see ships with the Republican flag approaching the palace. They have the cannons aimed toward the palace. They will bomb it, for certain."

"What are you talking about? Show me!" Manuel said, standing up.

The butler took him by his hand and led him to the top floor, where there was a spyglass in a pavilion made especially for observation.

"You are right," Manuel spoke urgently.   "I think I begin to understand everything. Mother is in Belem. She must be warned. She should head for Mafra!"

"She will be informed, Your Majesty! Everything is ready!"

In her beloved palace, Amelie was sitting with a cup of tea, already cold. When the servant announced the arrival of Angelo, the old and faithful servant, she understood what was happening.

"Madame," he bowed, "your son, still the King, orders you to go immediately to the Mafra Palace to meet him. There is no time! Betrayal is near. I cannot stay, for the King wants me back. There is a carriage waiting for you in the back, which will take you, unseen. The coup is beginning is on the water. You can hear the cannon fire. They are bombing the King's palace. To Mafra, Madame! I'm leaving now."

Angelo, like a ghost, vanished from sight. Amelie, with difficulty, convinced Maria Pia to get in the carriage to go to Mafra. Fortunately, her *dame de compagnie*, her official companion, was there. Lisbon was quiet; one could see only a few people in the streets.

"That insurgence does not have the support of the masses," Amelie said hesitantly.

"What insurgence?" the old Queen asked.

"The exile, Madame. They are bombing the King's palace. We shall meet Manuel in Mafra Palace, and tomorrow we are leaving for England."

31

"To England? And what shall we do there? Portugal is our country!" Maria Pia cried.

"It was and still will be for one more night; then it is all over. That's why we went to your son's grave."

Maria Pia said no more. They reached the Mafra Palace and left the carriage near a private entrance, where a door opened and closed rapidly. It was Era Angelo. No more cannon blasts could be heard, a sign that the revolutionaries had entered the palace. When she saw Angelo, Amelie was greatly relieved, for that was a sign that Manuel was there, in that dark hunting palace, seldom visited by ladies.

"Thank God he's safe!" she said. The king received them distractedly.

"Now they are declaring the republic in Palacio de Necesidades," he said, without smiling. "I am no longer King!"

"But you are alive!" said Amelie, "And this is what matters."

"What, you are no longer King?!" Maria Pia shouted, remaining shocked for a while.

"No, I am only a simple citizen," he told his grandmother. "But they don't have people gathered in front of the Court of Law. People don't like traitors and those taking power by force, which is also a kind of dictatorship, a kind of Franco. When I left there, they hadn't started bombing yet. From the pavilion, one could see them drawing near slowly, obscenely, toward the palace. I had only enough time to pick some flowers which I am going to keep, to take one more look at Joao V's bust, and those gardens of exotic plants that I enjoyed all alone when I had nothing to do. But let's sit in the parlor. They won't look for us; they are too enthusiastic about what they have done."

The family sat down, and Maria Pia took her medicines, for she needed them. She fell asleep in the armchair. Amelie stood up and looked around the room. She had never liked Mafra with all those trophies on the walls. It looked sinister, and the sunlight never came in as it did in Belem. She was waiting in anticipation for the signal from her son to leave forever. These past two years, she had passionately hated Portugal; it was the cross she had to bear.

Manuel finally came out of the room and started walking in the palace unlit by a source that would easily brighten the place. There was only the light coming in through the windows, but that was too little. He crossed the galleries filled with animal heads displayed on the walls in a striking exhibition. His mother's sad smile appeared when she crossed the aisle between the two royal apartments. It is said that the King announced

32

his coming to the Queen with the sound of a trumpet – this is how great the distance was between the two apartments.

"How funny these kings were in the past, and I am not even married!" the young man thought.

The wind moving the tree branches reminded him of the legends told in relation to that palace. In fact, every imposing building had its stories. He started laughing a bit to himself when he thought about the superstitions related to the sewage network of the palace. They said that at night, huge rats would come out from the canals, killing and devouring those occupying the building if they found them anywhere but in bed.

"Ha, ha, where are you? Why don't you jump on my back to tear me apart?" he asked. "Portuguese people, superstitious as Catholics! None of this is true," he went on talking, stumbling over a step. He stopped talking to himself.

He sat down on the stairs and thought of his brother who had passed away in such a terrible way, so young.

"Luis," he spoke, "a gardener cannot be a king., You were so wrong. I know you're watching me from somewhere up there. What comes to my mind right now is your funeral and father's funeral, those carriages shrouded in black, your horse in black, too, that bulk of crowns, those flowers cut for no good reason and faded away, the people standing on the roofs, in balconies, by the windows. I could have gotten killed, too. The guard could not possibly have handled it, he just couldn't, but maybe it was my bandaged hand that saved me. Do you know what happened to your horse? They shot him, so as to get to you sooner! Maybe you can ride up there on the clouds, who knows? And now, I'm running away from Portugal! I am no longer King. I don't want to die! I've had enough! Gaby isn't here, either., Who knows what show she has! But I shall see her soon. And grandmother, who lost her mind…. We leave you in Lisbon, Luis! I hope that your grave will not be profaned. Mafra has something black in her sky, something that gives me chills."

Toward the morning, Manuel was awakened from the stairs.

"Your Majesty, the ship is ready. The ladies are waiting for you to set toward Ericeira while it is still dark," the good servant said.

"Thank you. I'm ready," Manuel said.

"Where have you been?" his mother shouted when she saw him so pale.

"Mother, Mafra is indeed a palace of ghosts, but let's go…."

They climbed into the carriage taking them to the hidden ship, full of cherished things which they didn't want to leave behind. They got on

33

board and they set off at once They were free. It seems that Mafra had been watched and somebody had raised the alarm. One could hear shots coming from the bank aimed at their ship.

"Too late!" Manuel cried, without being heard. The captain ordered the departure at full speed, the swiftest speed that the ship was capable of. Bullets fell harmlessly in the water

"I shall live to damn you!" he cried when the Portuguese coasts were still visible.

A crowd of people had gathered that day, the 5th of October. They were watching the escape of the man who had been the King. The exile. The ship stopped only in Gibraltar, to wait for the fights to end between the monarchists in Porto and their Republican adversaries. When they learned the outcome, they boarded the ship again and set off to England forever, to the place where Amelie had been born and where she never dreamed of returning. Once they reached Portsmouth, they had only one small misunderstanding. The Queen Mother, Maria Pia, refused to remain in England. She wanted to go to her home in Italy.

"I want to die at home and be buried with my people," she said. "Sail the ship toward my dear Italy! I want to go to Torino. You, Amelie, you have reached your home. I want the same thing."

No one could talk Maria Pia out of her desire. After the captain provided the ship with all the necessary supplies for that unscheduled journey, they sailed for Italy; After this voyage, they would return to England and go to Fulwell Park.

They were very well received by King George V, who understood the aged Queen's feelings. The exile of her grandson had been the last straw. Her mind had been shattered forever. Goodbye, Portugal! Welcome to Torino! ... or London, for the other members of the family. Everything was ready at Amelie's house, only the weather was so bad, nothing like the heat of Portugal.

They learned about the declaration of the Portuguese Republic and the change of the state anthem. It was the first republic and it was led by Teofilo Braga, chairman of the interim government, former deputy of Lisbon. Manuel put the newspaper down, looking outside the window at the small, fine rain that wouldn't cease. A fire was burning in the fireplace, making the atmosphere all the more pleasant. He was alone. He gazed out at the park in front of him, which looked dreary because of the rain and fog. It was over. He would live for himself from now on.

Amelie received a letter confirming that Maria Pia had arrived safely in Torino and that she felt happy to be back. She too was now at her home, and she tried to enjoy it, even if she felt like a baby who had to accept the idea that her ball had been taken away and that she wasn't allowed to have dessert at dinner.

CHAPTER 5

For the Christmas holidays, the King of England invited them to the palace to enjoy Christmas and New Year's Eve. They decided to go even though Amelie thoroughly disliked the idea.

"Mother," her son told her one day, when they were all alone, I too want the Restoration, but that does not mean I stop living. If I am not King anymore, I'll not die; I'll write, I'll read, and I'll play tennis. I will not, at any rate, close down within myself, showing the whole world my defeat and my suffering. We must act normally, party if we are invited to party, and live our life with its small joys. We shall go, Mother, and you will shine with the diadem of our dynasty House. I shall wear all my decorations, and we shall be proud of Portugal. I swore I would respect my country, and I shall respect it, even if it is under a different form of leadership."

"You've become a philosopher and a strategist," Amelie of Orleans replied. "That is true; if the Portuguese wanted a republic, at least let us hope it will do them good, but something tells me it will not be like that. I still find it hard to accept this fall, but I shall follow your advice, my dear Manuel. We are going to celebrate with your friend, George. He is also in his first year of reign, but how solid the structures of the English monarchy are!"

"You forget about Oliver Cromwell and his Republic," Manuel quickly answered her. "Nothing is what it seems, nothing is solid, and it can all fall down anytime, even though I agree with you. Indeed, there is a major difference between Portugal and the United Kingdom. But I can attribute that to the fact that ordinary Portuguese people were interested and enthusiastic about the new regime, which changed the monarchy. The Lusitanians are somehow careless and inconsiderate, waiting for God to give them everything, which is a mistake. The English are not like that.

The Lusitanians sing *fado*, cry and live by it, saying that this is what God wanted. I love my people just the way they are. It is not those people that killed my father and Luis, but some sick minds that will not lift up the country from the chaos it is in. But let's not talk about this anymore. A new year is about to begin, and I do hope it will be a better one. I'm sorry grandmother is not here with us. She was so disappointed because of my losing the throne that she doesn't want to see me again. I think I cause her pain and remembrance."

"Maria Pia's mind has been terribly shaken. I think that the only solid thing remaining from her whole life is her first home: Torino. There she can find her peace, for she was born there. I was born here, but it seems I still need time to digest these events, which happened so quickly. And then, look at this abysmal weather ! How will I ever get used to it? Where is the sun over Tejo? It's very difficult for me to look outside the window at the park where I played when I was a child."

"You'll learn to love England again, remembering your childhood," Manuel assured her.

"Ah, I forgot to tell you. Today we have a guest at lunch: the vicar from the St. James Church, which Fulwell belongs to. We'll have to attend the Christmas Mass, so probably the vicar is coming to wish us welcome and tell us that we are expected."

"That is good, mother! I'm glad. It is really a good thing that he is coming and that we have a Roman Catholic church near us. Also, this man will give us the news in the area, and I don't think he is a morose man. I shall be there at noon. I think I'll go now; I want to look over the library. I'll read whatever I can find. I don't see what else I can do in such weather."

At lunch, the guest proved to share the King's way of thinking. He was talkative and open-minded. They spoke a bit about the unfortunate situation they were in, but, on that subject, Manuel answered:

"My heart will always beat for the country where I was born, and I shall always accept what is done politically, even if I differ. I swore on the Constitution. I am a patriot, even if from distance, and that says it all."

The vicar nodded with understanding; then in the end, he invited them to the Christmas Mass and every Sunday to his small, old church. The Queen thanked him for his visit and promised that they would be there. When the vicar's carriage could be heard on the stone driveway, she exhaled with relief, stating that he was a pleasant man, but too talkative.

At the ball held at the palace, those two, mother and son, truly shone, and did not let anyone, not even for a moment, see defeat on their faces. Both of them danced and conducted themselves so as to merit

37

everyone's praise. Manuel made friends and they decided to meet at a famous fencing room to exercise their wrists. The young ladies were keeping their eyes on that handsome dethroned King. But Manuel was not interested in contracting a marriage. He danced with everyone with no favoritism, but his heart remained all his own. He had such a wonderful time, something he had not done in a long time, and everybody enjoyed his light spirit and his good mood. They probably expected to see something else, but the king was resplendent in his military attire on which shone all the decorations and medals he had received.

They did not stay until the end of the party, but left in full glory, as they would put it, thus giving everyone the chance to make favorable comments about them. In the morning, they were to honor the invitation to the Mass, as they had promised the vicar.

When she entered the church, she recalled the many masses she had attended as a child. Nothing had changed. Everything – the benches, the paintings with the Stations of the Cross, the statues – everything had remained the same. She felt as if she were a little girl again, receiving Holy Communion, wearing a white dress with a flower crown on her head. They went to "our places," as Amelie considered them. Actually those were the usual places of the Orleans. Nothing had changed. The prayers books were still on the benches. At first, many people watched them as though they were genuine rarities, but then the congregation became accustomed to seeing them there every Sunday.

"I liked being at the church," Amelie commented over lunch. "It was wonderful to turn back time. I can see myself with my dear mother on the church pew. But these are my own private thoughts. What are you doing today?"

"Today I shall stay in the greenhouse. There are a lot of interesting things to see in there. The plants are very well cared for, and there are some species I don't know. Did you know I received a letter from Gaby? She will come to London in spring. I can't wait to see her. Her conduct was exemplary while I was King."

"You must get married, son," the Queen said, sighing.

"I know, but I can't think of anyone, and I won't make another try with English princesses. I don't want another rejection. I saw that quite a few of the young ladies at the ball, were looking at me warmly, but in vain. I've made up my mind: I do not want an English woman! Anyway, we will have another chance to be at King George's court right on the New Year's Eve, and you will realize that it would be better to have someone besides an English lady. I've made some friends with whom I'll soon go to a respectable fencing room. I haven't done that in a while, and I miss handling the sword. Now, this is what I am thinking about."

"If you received a letter from Paris, well, you should know that I received a letter from Italy. Your grandmother is sick; she is more and more sick. She has had a nervous breakdown, and her mind rests with difficulty, and then thanks only to the medicines. And now, when she has moments of lucidity, she cries over the loss of Portugal and your removal from the throne. You see, she no longer has the vigour of your hopes for a better future. She's living in her memories. She is still a Queen, and she cannot realize what you've come to accept so easily. I don't feel good either when I think about it, but your youth gives me wings and faith in a better future. My brother-in-law, the Duke of Porto, visits her from time to time, but he doesn't stay for too long. Afonso is morose and irritable. I can't even imagine why he hasn't got married yet. I don't think that is such an ideal relationship between mother and son. He lives in Naples instead of living with her in Torino. Who knows what he's doing there. He likes it that way; he cannot be away from the Mediterranean."

After the meal, the two embraced each other tenderly. Manuel kissed his mother's hand, and went to the greenhouse, where the gardener was already waiting for him. The air in the greenhouse was warm and musty, which the King was used to. He saw many of the plants he had spoken to his mother about, amazing the gardener with his knowledge. He liked the orange trees, which grew freely in his country. They were small, but well cared for. They gave plenty of fruit, but made him long for the gardens of the royal palace in Lisbon. He shook himself and continued to busy himself with the small plants that didn't harm anyone, but on the contrary, brought only joy.

Let's leave the inhabitants in Fulwell for a while to enjoy their peace and hopes for the future, and go to Piemont, in Torino, where the Queen Mother stared blankly, as was her unfortunate sad habit, sitting in an armchair by the window in her room. She fiercely refused to do anything else all day long. She was dreadfully unhappy during the end of that year. Only when her personal priest came did she seem to come back to her senses, and then she would begin crying. Then lucid, she would tell him:

"Father, Manuel is young. He can still hope for something in his life, maybe my daughter-in-law, Amelie, too, but for me that was too much, to run away like a thief from the country whose Queen I had been for so many years. I cannot regain my peace. In my mind, I see all the time the faces of my son and my grandson lying there lifeless in Palacio de Necesidades among flowers. I was there, in that carriage. Why didn't any of the bullets touch me? I was sixty years old, my life was already in its twilight."

"My daughter," the old priest told her, "just like the Queen, we should not ask such questions. God wanted them martyrs, and that is what they are. This was their fate, and we who are still here must accept this fate and pray for them."

"I would like to go to them, Father! I think I will soon. This is what I feel," the Queen confessed.

"We must not trouble God. He knows when we have to go to Him."

"Also, Father, I don't like this weather. It is not warm here; the mountains are close, and my bones ache because of the cold, no matter how warm it might be in the rooms. I have forgotten the time when I used to play in the palace park, but I do not wish to go back to Portugal; I want to be buried here in my family's chapel. I hate the country that exiled me and from which I left like a thief, with the bullets of those reprobates exploding around our ship."

Maria Pia had grown tired after so much rationality. She lay her head on the armchair and started gazing again the way she always did. She had once more entered her own world from which she would come out so seldom. She had closed her eyes and fallen asleep. The priest made the sign of the cross and withdrew. Her *dame de compagnie* entered her room, put a quilt across her legs, and went out slowly, leaving the door half-closed.

"She is suffering a great deal," the priest whispered as he walked to the carriage.

"Unfortunately, she will never be a Queen again," her friend sighed, kissing the priest's hand. "Please do come back; I think your company comforts her."

"I will come again for certain," he said, again making the sign of blessing, and then the sign for the carriage to set off.

During those times in London, Manuel, who had made many friends, was in a fencing room for the first time since he arrived on the island. He was laughing and telling his friends that he hadn't yet gotten in shape and that he felt as if he had a shield on him because of the lack of exercise. He enjoyed fencing very much; it truly relaxed him. His friends were not especially fit either, but they promised to come often to the room to practice. They were all waiting for 1911 and its fireworks as well as the champagne that would flow abundantly and the good mood of people like themselves, rich and carefree. These English noblemen whom Manuel joined did not have his desires to return to the Lusitanian throne, or at least

40

to see their country without those spasmodic crises which Portugal had experienced. Manuel was a true patriot, with his soul far away toward that land full of sun which he had left so quickly.

On New Year's Eve, he and his mother drank a glass of champagne for Portugal, for its salvation. They stayed at the Court festivities until midnight, then vanished from sight. It was already 1911; they had nothing left to wait for. They went in peace and quiet to their apartments where they went to sleep with the crackling of a fire in the fireplace, the customary fireplaces in British houses. Then, they had problems to think of. They had received news from the Portuguese royalists, who wanted the Restoration. Manuel wanted that, of course, but legitimately and without bloodshed. But he did not have the passion which his grandmother from Torino, for instance, would have wanted him to have, probably because he was young and free, and – let us not forget – he had not been raised to be a king.

He wanted to be a king – there was no doubt about that – but peacefully and fully accepted by his people, not as his reign had been, a ceaseless fight between cat and mouse. He did not see that acceptance coming from the Republicans. They already had the reins of authority and the feverish desire to rule. The thirst for power was supreme. He was certain that Teofilo Braga would not wait with flowers for him to get off the ship, and that he would never hand over to him the leadership of the country. Such a thing would never happen.

He also believed that his royalists would instigate attacks, and there would be blood again in the streets of Portugal's capital. That was what scared him. He hated the blood and the dead on the pavement. He had not forgotten that beginning of 1908. How could he forget? He was horrified by violent clashes and gunfire, shooting only out of vanity or because of any deranged motive. He preferred his exile and the prosperity of Portugal to war in the streets and squares of Lisbon.

Manuel was what he was, a pacifist who complied with his vow to uphold the Constitution of the country where he had been born.

CHAPTER 6

The most interesting and simultaneously the most intriguing news which the Portuguese King received in 1911 was that his monarchists, the ones supporting him, had located their camp in Galicia, Spain. Manuel was astonished that the Spanish, their leadership in particular, accepted that crowd of people on their territory. In his reply letter, he urged peaceful and legal methods to restore the monarchy in Portugal. Instead, the churning and impatience of those in the Galician camp credited that perspective and desire of the sovereign to his youth, and did not give it much consideration. It seemed their interest was mostly toward their own ends, and Manuel was rather a puppet. Their leader, Henrique Conceiro, in reply to Manuel's letter inquiring about his tactics, financial resources, and other such important elements, replied that they would manage with little and would succeed. Manuel was disheartened and brought the same mood to his mother's soul.

"I'm afraid they've got only a bag of enthusiasm and nothing else. They don't even know what they rely on, and unfortunately they will not listen to the man they want to be their leader. They will not succeed, no matter how optimistically they might be in their thinking. I received the newspaper they publish in Galicia. It's just food for the soul, but for a restoration, you need money, a lot of money, you need an army and coldblooded leaders, not dreamers."

"We shall wait," Amelie answered. "What can we do from here?"

What the exiled King foresaw came true. Conceiro's plan was to raise the peasants to fight, ignorant peasants who did not understand anything and did not react in any way. The lack of money, the lack of an army led with strength and cunning as well as flawless tactics caused Conciero's incursion to fail miserably. His forces returned back to Galicia, to the distress of the Spanish in the area.

Manuel regretted deeply that lack of provision and subsequently the loss of that opportunity. He had tried to help, but his resources were limited. Besides that news, they received another one in that first year of exile. Queen Maria Pia would no longer get out of bed; she was resigned, waiting for her end. They left to go to Torino while she was still living., She passed away immediately after seeing them. They buried her just as she had wanted, in her family's Pantheon. The fear of Portugal followed her into death. She was the Queen who did not want a place in the Braganza family Pantheon. After all, what difference did it make? Afonso, her unmarried son, came, too, and after the ceremony, they went their separate ways. The Queen was 64 and had suffered enough, as the people who cared for her when she returned home were saying. She had been a Queen of social causes, but also of conspicuous luxury.

The only pleasant moments during that time were the tours of Gaby in London, which also ended badly. During their last meeting, the beautiful actress announced to the King her definite departure to the United States, with a view to building her career. That was a blow to Manuel. He liked Gaby, liked her discretion and her frankness, but he would lose her. Actually, he had already lost her, and he was single again. Losing Gaby hurt Manuel, but he knew he had to go on. He really needed to get married, but didn't feel quite ready yet.

The year of 1911 was a year full of events, of meetings with friends, of long prayers at the parish church. The most sincere friend proved to be the very King George who truly loved Manuel. They met quite often, when George had some spare time, and their difference in age didn't matter. In fact, that never matters in a true friendship.

Manuel greatly enjoyed fencing, and he improved his technique considerably thanks to his practicing. He loved writing, and his dream was to write a book about the glorious age of Portugal. To that aim, he researched intensely and gathered an abundance of materials. Tennis was another passion of his, and he played at Wimbledon for the first time since he had been in exile. Manuel was always next to his mother, always with a smile on his lips, and always displaying his Portuguese decorations. He was proud to wear them. He could see the ordeal of the Portuguese to rise up from the political mire, but he could only watch helplessly from a distance. Anywhere he went, he was received with kindness and much consideration. That was the first year in exile of that King with a heart as big as his country.

Manuel received continual updates of what was going on with his royalist forces in Spain. They were organizing a new incursion in their country, thinking they were very well prepared from every perspective;

and time proved them to be correct. But with all their improved organization, the result was the same as with their first incursion over the border. Moreover, on this occasion, the Spanish government disarmed the Portuguese and shut down their newspaper from the exile in an attempt to stabilize and secure the area.

Manuel sent them one more letter in which he repeated that he wanted the reign legitimately, without force and bloodshed. But the King was young and was thus ignored.

In 1912, Manuel attended an event in Switzerland where he met a young lady, a German princess, who made him return to London a bit affected. Once home, he began gathering information about her with the help of some trustworthy people. Her name was Augusta Victoria, an interesting young woman with blonde hair and blue eyes. She was a member of the ruling House of Hohenzollern, and she was the niece of King Ferdinand I of Romania. When he told his mother about Augusta, she welcomed the news gladly.

"I would be so happy if you married! I think she is a remarkable young lady, and you would be married within the family. I shall go one day to the palace and ask the Queen of our good King George about that subject, keeping it all a secret, of course. I think Mary of Teck will provide me with more information about this German princess."

When she decided to go, Amelie was warmly received by Queen Mary, and when it comes to arranging marriages, women are peerless. Mary learned all the information about Augusta and wholeheartedly recommended her for Manuel.

The young King was also glad to hear the news about the princess whom he liked so much. There was no comparison between her and Gaby. After a year, he had forgotten her. He decided to write an official letter proposing to his blonde cousin, but he delayed that pleasant activity for duty to his country called. He had received an official letter from Miguel II, son of King Miguel I, the one who had usurped the throne of Maria II, and then abdicated in her favor. Miguel II asked for a meeting with the last King of Portugal, with reference to the succession within the House of Braganza. In response, Manuel prepared and wrote also an official letter in which he stated his agreement, but also expressed his perplexity, for he could at any point get married and have children, which would subsequently cancel any desire Miguel II might have had.

In the ensuing correspondence, they established a meeting in Dover, the beautiful entry harbor from France. Amelie agreed to the meeting, but did not go to that Victorian city, leaving it all in her son's hands. Dover is an attractive harbor framed by white chalk rocks,

44

dominated by the huge castle built in the 12th century by Henry II. So much history and so many secrets reside in that building full of mysterious tunnels. As long as he stayed there, Manuel was thrilled to explore freely, at ease and without company on the bank of the English Channel.

When Miguel II arrived and they met officially, they were truly glad. But then the former King cut him off when his relative began to express his compassion toward Manuel's fate:

"I'm fine, trust me. I am just sorry that such a harsh act won't bring peace. These Republicans want power for themselves, but they did not take the people into account at all. In fact, I think you know that there have been two attempts at restoration, which the lower classes did not react to. And not because they don't love me, but because this is how they are. They turn their attention only as far as their yard goes."

"I'm so glad you have such a good outlook," Miguel II said. "The latter, we should remind ourselves, are supported by the Lusitanian Integralist Party."

"Yes. The Queen sends you greetings and wants you to know she is sorry she couldn't come to Dover. It's beautiful here," the king said, looking around and changing the subject. "One can have a really good tea here," he smiled.

"We taught them to drink tea," Dom Miguel said, with his fists clenched.

"Maybe, but now it doesn't matter. We're going down, anyway, with or without tea," Manuel said, sadly.

"That's why I wanted us to meet, son, not to go down. My wish is that the House of Braganza would overcome the years and survive," the old man answered, sighing.

"And what do you want? Succession to the governance of our House in case I get married and die without having heirs? Your being entrusted with the rights that your father lost and for which he was exiled? I can do that, and I will do it, but I tell you honestly that I don't believe so much anymore in Restoration. I know my people. I repeat this: they have their own concerns, they pay taxes irrespective of who rules the country."

"You are right, that is true, but I would like to have my rights back, just as you said. And my son, in the event of an unfortunate situation, which I do not wish, I would follow you as Duke of Braganza. Do not think I am sly and that I attack you, like a fox. No. I just want to carry on our name and house. I want to unite the branches of the House of Braganza."

"Duarte Nuno? Certainly, why not? This very evening, I shall draw up a paper that I shall hand to you tomorrow. We are staying at the same hotel, so it is very convenient. I repeat, I no longer believe in royalty in Portugal. Four years ago, I went through a tragedy from which I learned a great deal. Had I been an ordinary man, my father and my brother Luis would be alive now. I have forgotten nothing. Peace is the most precious jewel, the family peace, I mean. Mother foresaw the goal of this visit of yours to England, and supports this branch of our House with all her heart. You will have all your rights, even the one pertaining to succession, if I die without heirs. It is somewhat amusing, because I am only 23, but I shall write the paper, for the peace of this House."

"Thank you, Manuel," Dom Miguel said, taking the King's hands into his own. "You are a genuine Braganza and you have understood my gesture as such, without hidden thoughts."

"It's odd, anyway. What I would be interested in is what may happen after my soul goes to heaven or rests on a flower in my greenhouse. And, besides, there's still my mother. What if she lives a hundred years? She will be the head of the House then, and you will have to ask her."

They finished their meal together and then went to see the ocean. Everything was so beautiful. In the morning, Dom Miguel received the document whereby he was re-entrusted with all his rights, and all of the "Miguel" branch of the House of Braganza came back under his auspices. Duarte Nuno was now Manuel's heir, in case he were not to have children, and thus everything ended. Upon his departure, Dom Miguel had tears in his eyes, thanking the King because he had forgiven and removed his father's mistakes. Manuel smiled at him, and thus that important event for the future of the House of Braganza ended.

"Get married and have children!" the old man shouted at him from the deck of the ship that would soon cross the English Channel.

When it vanished from sight, Manuel exhaled in relief and prepared to go home, to do what he had planned to do before being interrupted by his relative. He wanted, if you recall, to write to Prince Wilhelm in Germany and ask him for his daughter's hand in marriage. He was looking forward to returning to London. Also, he missed his mother, whom he had never left alone during all these months.

CHAPTER 7

On his way back, he realized that Dom Miguel, his uncle, was right. Duarte Nuno was a child with all of his future lying ahead of him, and their Dynasty House was covered if he himself did not have heirs.

He was very glad when he reached home. His mother came to meet him, asking about that meeting. She was pleased with the document that her son had issued; the reintegration into their rights of the heirs of the usurping King Miguel I was just. In fact and *de jure*, Miguel I was of royal blood, in spite of what he did, illegally reigning in Portugal, imposing unnecessary terror. Amelie was not at all interested in upcoming reactions – which in fact, she anticipated – of the other branches of the Braganza House. Those branches, auxiliary and distant, were not so important.

Manuel knew very well how to write and thus to compose an official letter in flattering terms. He could hardly wait to sit down at his desk, and when he finished the letter, he was thoroughly content. Princess Augusta had stolen his heart. He sent his missive, along with his hopes, through an official courier and then waited. He imagined how long it would take to get from one place to the other, and how long it would be before the German prince had the letter in his hands. His reaction, Augusta's reaction, everything was played out in his mind. He must be successful; they were related and also close in age.

In the meantime, he passed the time in the fencing room or riding around.

Finally he received the long awaited reply, and that reply was favorable. Wilhelm blessed the alliance, and Augusta obviously agreed to it. They had a special invitation for the winter holidays to the Prince's castle, which they accepted immediately. Probably their engagement would take place then, they said to each other. He knew that his mother, the Queen, would take care of the jewels, so that, elated, he was trying to contain his excitement until mid-December. The Queen was also cheerful, and she loved being involved in the planning of the event. Queen Mary too was glad of the success of the negotiations.

"A truly matching pair," she said, congratulating Amelie. "They will be happy; the princess has a very peaceful and serene nature, just like Manuel. Bravo! I must also tell this good news to my husband George; this will put him in a fine state of mind."

They had had new clothes made especially for this much wanted engagement. He was the only son of Amelie to marry. Sometimes she would close her eyes and see the graves of her husband and her son next to one another, and then melancholy would seize her. But she would quickly rise out of it. She could not bring them back to see Manuel's wedding, no matter how much she wanted that.

They left for Sigmaringen, a wonderful castle, set like any castle, on a mountainside. Once they reached the continent, the farther inland they advanced, the heavier the snow until the thick layer became a permanent element in the landscape. They were not used to the cold, but the scenery was breathtaking and made them forget the inconveniences of the road.

They were magnificently received by Prince Wilhelm himself and his entire Court. Augusta made the same impressions on him as during their previous encounter in Switzerland. She was beautiful, blonde, and undemanding. She smiled at Manuel as soon as she saw him, and her bow before his mother was perfect. Her blonde hair was styled in a simple hairdo which emphasized her lovely eyes. As for her outfit, no one remembered that, not the King, at any rate, who was entranced simply by her eyes. They were shown the apartments where they would stay. The view from the windows was stunning; it was as if they were in an eagle nest, but luxurious and warm.

"I have always thought that these castles would be cold and unaccommodating because of their thick walls and inability to preserve the heat, but I was wrong," Manuel said to his mother when he met her to go to lunch.

Amelie had prepared the jewels for her son's engagement and she immediately took his arm and went downstairs. The engagement party was very intimate and thoroughly prepared. There were just a few people, which truly pleased the Queen. Augusta wore a blue dress which fell beautifully on her slender body. She was truly lovely, and Manuel was happy.

"Let's have the wedding next autumn, here at the castle," Prince Wilhelm said. "The castle will be decorated specially for this event. What do you say?"

"An excellent plan," Manuel said. "It's beautiful here, an interesting dwelling, all perched here on this huge rock."

"You should see the fireworks on the Danube on the New Year's Eve! A splendour! I will never forget them," Augusta said, blushing.

"Do you like the jewels?" Amelie asked.

"Very much. The House of Braganza has truly magnificent jewels."

"We are glad that you like them; wear them with joy," Amelie said.

"Let's toast these young people who will unite their destinies," Prince Wilhelm cried. "May death be the only thing that will ever separate these two; may they understand each other by looking at one another, and may they be happy!"

Everybody shouted that typical German salutation "Heil!" They clinked their glasses and applauded. The two young people, hand in hand, stood there excited, receiving congratulations. The wedding was set for the following year in early September. So many things had to be prepared! During that month, it would be pleasant on the Danube, not yet cold.

Through that holiday, Manuel realized even more that he had not been wrong about his bride-to-be. She showed him the whole castle, which was quite different from what it had been before being rebuilt. It had burned, and restoration began, at enormous cost, in 1893.

Manuel loved the lofty exposure of the castle, right above the shining blue Danube. He was enchanted by the Portuguese Gallery of the palace which Augusta showed him, laughing at his astonishment at finding bits of his own country there. What he loved most were the fireworks on the Danube at midnight on the New Year's Eve. They were already in 1913, and Manuel had stolen the first kiss from his fiancée. They both had much to meditate on. They were very much in love, to their wonder and that of everyone else. When Manuel left to return to England, they promised to write to each other as often as they could, and Augusta asked Manuel for two more meetings before their wedding; of course he gladly accepted. Prince Wilhelm was pleased about his beloved daughter's courage and gladly approved the invitation conveyed by his daughter. Wilhelm's mother, Antonia, Augusta's grandmother, Infanta of Portugal, was thrilled. Antonia was 67 at the time, and the fact that the wedding would take place at the castle was a blessing for her. She didn't often go out from the castle, and she hoped she would live to see her granddaughter marry a Portuguese relative of hers. Sadly, Augusta's mother was no longer alive; she had passed away a few years before. She had been a very beautiful woman, Princess Maria Teresa de Bourbon-Two Sicilies. She left behind three very beautiful children, Augusta and her two brothers, who would inherit the title. The elder brother was Friedrick, the presumptive ruler of the House, but considering the misfortune of the royal family in Portugal, nothing was a certainty anymore.

When they separated from each other, everyone felt unhappy, but Manuel promised he would make two more visits to Baden Wurttemberg before September, when the wedding was set. And of course letters would flow from both ends, with Prince Wilhelm's approval, of course.

Once they arrived home, in their foggy and rainy land, mother and son had a long discussion.

" Son," Amelie said, "I've been thinking a lot lately. When you come here with your wife, when you live here, we must live in different places." Seeing a gesture of discontent from Manuel, she continued, "Do not interrupt me. I have thought this through, and I have decided not to give in to your insistence. I shall go to the Duke of Orleans, in my father's country. You shall come and visit me, and I shall receive you with much love. But I wish to be alone with my thoughts. I have already sent a letter to this effect to France. Chateau de Bellevue will be ready in September to receive me. Everything ends for me with this marriage. As they would put it, you are flying from the nest. I know I wouldn't bother you, but I believe I need to live for myself, too. I am a strong person. I know this, but you see, strong people need to take a break, too. Please do not fight this, and try to understand as much as you can. I love you with all my heart. You are all I have left, and you know it will be hard for me to leave, but I must."

"Oh, mother, if this is what you wish, I shall abide by it. I can understand that you are seeking solitude, but allow me to tell you that France is not your country, but your father's. You are going to a foreign place, no matter how many roots might connect you to it. But go, I let you go, from my heart. But I shall visit you very often. I love Paris, my first love is linked to this city, and I believe that Augusta likes it, too. There's still time until September, so I won't think about it for now."

"Thank you, Manuel! Your sensibilities have always understood mine. I wish you all happiness with your princess. I shall take great care of everything you may need, so that your wife will enjoy the house where I was born and will think kindly of the one who took care of its management, especially for the two newly married young people."

The two embraced. They loved each other so much! Manuel had no idea of the surprise his mother was going to make him, but he would learn that on his wedding day. Until then it would remain a secret.

In his visits to Sigmaringen, Manuel had walked along the Danube. He cast a more detailed look at the castle rooms, and walked around as he pleased in the forest, bringing Augusta Victoria all kinds of flowers, one more beautiful than the other. But what they liked most of all was to watch the Danube, together, from the castle perched on that impressive rock.

"Won't you feel sorry, Augusta, if you leave this view for London?" Manuel asked when they were alone on the terrace.

"No, I feel I can go with you anywhere. I don't know why, but I don't think it will make much difference. Anyway, we shall come here again, at least to see grandmother," she said, smiling and gently squeezing his hand.

"Do you know that after our wedding, my mother will move to France, to a castle near Versailles? So, one more reason to spend time on the continent. She will leave us to be alone. Now she is taking care of the management and necessary arrangement at Fulwell Park and she hopes that you will love it," Manuel went on.

"Yes? How thoughtful! Then I will love it twice as much. Anyway, time passes so quickly, and September will come soon. I am looking forward to it! There is a certain excitement in the castle. Father smiles when he sees me. The tailors are always around me, except for when you come and visit us. They are not allowed to disturb us then," she said laughing. "I just wish my mother could have been here. She would be so happy. But I cannot bring her back to life. My father is bearing his widowhood normally, like a man, which is another reason that I love him even more. He may remarry, who knows, but I won't begrudge him that. He loves us three so much, and now he loves you, too."

"Thank him for me for that affection," Manuel told her.

It was true; time passed quickly in favor of the bride and groom. Even Infanta Antonia's prayer was heard, and in September she was happily still living, waiting for the event. She watched the castle transforming, filling with flower garlands and, artful statues symbolizing love, and she also saw the groom and his mother arriving with their entourage a few days before the wedding. Crowned heads arrived at the castle as well, which promised a special event such as had not been in the castle for a long time. Of course they could not be stopped from discussing politics, closed in the prince's study. There, Manuel expressed his fears once again:

"I fear for my country. That Republic is so weak! I am afraid that their weakness will bring about foul consequences for Portugal. Whatever may happen, I remain a Portuguese until the very end, irrespective of where my house is."

Everybody approved him. The bloodshed in 1908 had not been forgotten, and it had caused problems in every country ruled by a monarchy. People present there appreciated his nationalist spirit and they thought, in a deep corner of their souls, that in a similar situation, they would do the same. What is certain is that they liked Manuel.

The surprise that Amelie arranged for her son was that the religious wedding Mass was performed by Jose Neto, Cardinal of Lisbon, who was exiled in Spain. He had baptized Manuel. Indeed, this was an unexpected joy, for which the groom fervently thanked his mother. On the day of the wedding, everyone gathered at the castle chapel: members of the royal families from Spain, Germany, Italy, France, and Romania, for Princess Augusta was the niece of King Ferdinand I of Romania. Edward, Prince of Wales, was present, also.

The two days of celebration were perfect. Fireworks embraced the Danube in the night between the two days. It was a dreamlike wedding, and the bride and groom were young and beautiful. Augusta wore her family diadem, and Manuel wore all the decorations he had received and fully deserved. The honeymoon had been arranged to take place in Munich, and from there they would go to England. Everybody saw them off on their departure, and Manuel said goodbye to his mother with heartache. He knew he would visit her often in Paris; there was no other way. That was all they had left.

Indeed, after saying goodbye to their hosts, especially Antonia of Portugal, Amelie left for Paris. Her castle was waiting for her. That would be her home from then until the end of her life.

The two young people adjusted very well to their life together in Fulwell Park, and everything foretold a peaceful marriage. Only one event shadowed that year, namely the death of Augusta's grandmother. Antonia of Portugal had closed her eyes at the end of December, never to wake again. There had been dreadful weather during that distressing event, but no one stayed away. Everyone had loved her. She would be remembered always and would stay in their hearts forever. Following their return to London, the young couple resumed their peaceful life so much desired in a marriage.

CHAPTER 8

Amelie wrote often from Paris where she said she had been visited by the son of Miguel I. His little boy, Duarte Nuno, was a sweetness of a child. He was so funny. She was pleased for this child to be the righteous heir of the House in the unhappy event that Manuel would not have any children. Augusta had been a bit sick, but she recovered. They receive visits, and in their house they would hold parties where the London gentlefolk were received with much consideration.

Nobody had forgotten about Portugal, but life went on. There were great balls held with a view to obtaining funds for different charity activities which the former King patronized. Manuel loved the community of the St. James parish where he had ordered and donated a stained glass window with the coat of arms of the House of Braganza. He was a practising Catholic, and the people who had looked at him with awe at first were now growing to like him and his beautiful wife. They even served as godparents for children in the parish church, to the delight of everybody around. They very much wanted to feel integrated and accepted by the community, and that wish came true, for they were greeted and respected everywhere.

Manuel continued his activities, which he had learned in his childhood as a Duke of Beja. He played tennis, he went to the fencing room, he went riding when the weather allowed, and always he was thinking about his beloved Portugal. He knew that the monarchists would not give in so easily, and that they would soon take action with new forces. It had been two years since they were rousted from Galicia, and they had been quiet and peaceful for too long. So the time was ripe for some new action.

The royalists were pleased that the King had a beautiful wife and they imagined a lovely re-coronation ceremony. Dom Manuel smiled when reading the news he received from the camp that was loyal to him. The King pleaded for peace, especially since the unrest that led to the first war in Europe, having as an instigating pretext the assassination of the heir to the Austrian-Hungarian throne, Franz Josef. In Manuel's opinion, there were too many empires in the old Europe, and the ultimatum of Austro-Hungary given to the Serbian kingdom came only naturally, for the heir had been killed there. He didn't see the attack on Lisbon as appropriate, now when the water was troubled everywhere. But for the regalists, that was a real trump. Thus, they disregarded the King's pragmatic thinking and set off to assault the Republicans.

On the 20th of October, 1914, the latter, very eager and grim, had created panic and disorder in the streets. Manuel's fear regarding the dissolution of the State pressed on him more and more. He feared that Spain would attack Portugal again, for there were illustrative precedents in the past. The country could not be stabilized by those Republicans intoxicated with the blood of his family. He tried to quell the enthusiasm of his supporters, but that was impossible. Under the leadership of some passionate and reckless rulers, the monarchists continued their efforts in 1915, during the great World War, to remove the Republic.. Their actions were condemned by Manuel himself, who did not see anything auspicious in those revolts carried out in such uncertain times.

The regalists destroyed the monument of the Republican Party, so as to have for themselves a pretext to insurrect the masses and let the street fighting begin. Many people died or were wounded, most of them innocent bystanders. The regalists, weakly endowed, were defeated by the democrat Republicans and enlisted as illegitimate. Thus, the Republic took over, though it was weakened by the actions of the monarchists.

"I think the colonies will be lost if they continue to play at being an army, I mean those who support me. There is a war going on in Europe, and all they do is add fuel to the fire. Leaders change their ambassadors so often in the countries they are friendly with, that they exasperate the diplomats. And let us not forget that they also lack money, and I cannot help them very much. There may be solutions, but only after peace returns in Europe. We can't have it all at once. Who has time when a war is going on to acknowledge me, in the best case scenario of the restoration? Everybody is waiting, but I think this is a long-term war."

He said these things to his wife, with an expression of defeat on his face. She listened to him and tried to soothe him in different ways, but she could understand that love for the land where her husband was born was much stronger. Then, there was his mother, alone or almost alone in Paris, and letters took so long to pass between them. He did one

54

memorable thing in 1915 for his Portuguese people: he prepared his will. In case he did not have heirs, everything would go to the Republic, and thus to the Portuguese, provided the Lusitanian power would establish the Foundation of the House of Braganza, and his body be repatriated and interred in the House Pantheon next to his ancestors. Even in exile, he showed everyone that his love for the country at the other end of the old world remained constant; nothing would change that.

In reality, it didn't matter very much to him, for he did not have an heir from Augusta. He was living in times that he fully accepted and respected. He wanted peace and tranquility in Europe, as well as stability of the borders of his beloved country. Augusta loved him with all her heart, in that comfortable way that men need, but which not many truly appreciate. Not even his political views pertaining to the war would interest the Princess. He was the husband that she loved, whom God gave her, so why would it matter that he was an anglophile? His uncle in Romania proved also to be an anglophile. That didn't change anything, only maybe that her father, Wilhelm, was somewhat upset, but that didn't concern her.

Augusta loved walking and riding with her husband. Theirs was a fortuitous match, for they shared the same passions, except maybe for fencing, which in time of war, Manuel did not practice so much anymore. The King actively dedicated himself to the war; he asked the sympathizers of the monarchy to refrain from any other manifestations until the end of that ugly war. He did not want the restoration of monarchy under those brutal conditions; moreover, he asked to be enrolled in the army of Portugal, but the Republicans turned him down, to his disappointment. That refusal was possibly due, as well, to the Germanophile trend, which was embraced by the monarchist leaders. Who could know? Monarchists saw in that adhesion a channel for the restoration of monarchy, but the King was anglophile, which presented yet another obstacle.

During the war, Manuel took a job with the Red Cross, which disappointed this man who wanted to fight on the front line. He managed, however, to find other means of supporting the war effort. He visited hospitals; he held parties and other events in Fulwell Park to raise funds. He went to Paris where, besides visiting his mother, he brought some improvements to the Portuguese hospital, specifically to the operating room there. On his return to England, he created the orthopedics section of the Shepards Bush Hospital, which would be in operation until 1925, so that every soldier entering the hospital could be helped.

A particularly happy event occurred in their family during that time, namely, in 1917, the marriage of his uncle Afonso to a woman from

America, a morganatic marriage, with the prince thus losing the rights he inherited by birth. Nevada Stoody Hayes proved to be a lovely lady, so his uncle did not lose much by choosing her. An equally happy event took place in Augusta's family, too: in 1915, her father married again. The event took place in the same castle, but the wedding was not so extravagant, maybe also because of the war and the fact that bride and groom were no longer so young. Augusta's Adelgunde de Bavaria was over forty and her father a bit over fifty.

Those events were moments of relaxation, reunion, remembrance, and long walks to the castle of the princes of Hohenzollern, Sigmaringen. Amelie did not attend the wedding of Prince Wilhelm; she preferred keeping to herself. She would get visits from Miguel II and his son, Duarte Nuno, whom she spoiled as if he had been her own and herself young and beautiful, just as the old times in Vila Vicosa.

All those activities behind the front were reported to Manuel simultaneously with the ending of the war. King George V invited the exiled king of Portugal to the parade honoring the military who returned victorious at the end of that great war. Thus it was proved that Manuel was a fine strategist and had been on the winners' side. Now with peace having been being restored, he could think at ease, about his country and his throne, but he was to be disappointed again. We will see how in the next chapter.

CHAPTER 9

The celebrations for the end of the war had barely concluded when a stunning piece of news came from Portugal with the first newspapers. The action described as follows was one that the King did not know about. He learned it just like everyone else, by reading it.

In Portugal, that strip of land troubled for so long by various social movements and political turmoil, the President was Sidonio Pais, a Republican with rich experience in diplomacy, formerly a parliamentarian and minister of finance. He was an unusual man who wished intensely for a reconciliation between Republicans and monarchists under the same sunny skies of Portugal. They were all people of the same country. He was an individual who, through his approach, led to moderate action. He truly believed in bringing his people to understanding at the negotiating table. He held onto his goal until the last moment and never believed in the so discrepant divergences among Lusitanians. During his rule, he attempted a reconciliation with the regalists several times. In fact, he was assassinated doing that.

On the 14th of December, 1918, in the Rossio railway station, Pais was leaving to go to Porto to negotiate with royalists at the monarchic camp. He never completed his trip because he was killed in cold blood by one Jose Julio da Costa. The political crisis was relit with this ordered assassination. The Republicans kept control of the country, but were unable to prevent the forming of new monarchical forces in the North who took courage after Pais's assassination.

In 1919, the monarchists, led by Paiva Conceiro, considered that it was time to establish military occupation of the city of Porto. Thus in Porto, an interim government was established, a pro-regalist government, which was strongly defended by its supporters. We should mention here that the ordinary population, just as always, remained indifferent to that great political turmoil, uninterested in rising up against the government in Lisbon. There we see how well the King understood his people; the regalists dismantled the Republican National Guard and thus controlled the city.

In Lisbon, the confrontations between the two camps were strongly in the Republicans' favor. Regalists who were caught were sentenced to long imprisonment. In Porto, the Republican National Guard was restored, turning their guns against the regalists and re-installing the republic. Again many regalists were arrested and received heavy sentences.

The King learned all that by reading the newspapers, as previously mentioned. He who had always asked from his supporters peace and legality in all their actions, was dumbstruck by what happened.

"Augusta, read this! Look how they listen to me, the ones who want Portugal to become a kingdom again!" His lady read it too, and then sadly told her husband:

"I think, Manuel, that we have to look ahead, and not behind. I don't think that anything will ever happen regarding the royal type of governance of the country. There will never be a monarchy again in Portugal. These people don't listen to anyone – I mean to you," she corrected herself. "In fact, now, they're lying in prison, and you didn't even know what was happening there. They took action according to their own conscience, may God forgive them! You are not assimilated in any way to this regrettable action. I think that now you must direct your life toward what you learned when you were a child, never thinking of being a king. You are no longer King, and I think that the chance of restoring the monarchy disappeared simultaneously with these reckless and extremely bad actions, undertaken with no chance to win. All that bloodshed, all that misery! Such a shame! I shall long pray for this people singing sorrow so sadly and so carelessly at the same time. I wonder whether, in Paris, your mother has learned of these disastrous events, from which Portugal will never recover. I expect so," Augusta gave the answer herself. "I'm sorry, my darling. I shall always be there by your side, within your heart, shedding bitter tears."

The two embraced and remained like that for a while, by the fireplace that was drying out the permanent dampness of London, of England, of their refuge at Fulwell Park. Manuel went back to his study and sat down at his desk, which he had neglected lately. He was thinking about Miguel II and his son. They were supported by the Central Junta in Portugal while he was sustained by the one in the North, the one that destroyed everything by killing Sidonio Pais. It seemed that the two

58

branches reconciled, the branch of Maria II and the branch of the usurper Miguel I. After all, what difference did it make? Augusta was right; he must return to study, to anything else. No matter, he did not have any children and did not care about that, either. Duarte Nuno would succeed him, irrespective of how and which side of the House of Braganza supported him. He was tired and he was only thirty. His whole life lay in front of him.

So many parties, just as many dissensions – they all exhausted him, so that he thought he'd better give it all up. Anyway, 1919 had been an ugly year. Thank God it was passing, day after day. He would start to write, to read, to go and see new places, but especially he would love Augusta more and more every day for her kind and generous soul. She was his treasure, which he shared with no one. Holidays would come again, and they would go to Paris and Sigmaringen; they would be together, soul to soul. He loved Portugal, but she opposed distance, so he loved Portugal from far away, knowing there would never be a second reign, let alone a reign of Miguel II. Never.

His dear wife had written letters announcing their visit to those above the Danube, as well as to Queen Amelie. The answers of their hosts spoke of their longing, for they wanted to have them there as soon as possible. They had decided: they would spend Christmas in France and New Year's Eve in Sigmaringen. They knew there would be no fireworks, but the blue river was still there, running free.

In Paris, they went to the theater with Amelie of Orleans, who was so rarely seen in society. That was an opportunity for many people to pay her their respects. In fact, it wasn't cold either, and the Christmas Mass was very beautiful and touching.

Sometimes Augusta reproached herself for not being able to give her husband a child, because in that way all disputes over succession to the House of Braganza would be over, but when she confessed her regret to Manuel, she could see that he did not put great importance on that matter.

"I am happy with you, whether we have children or not," he replied soothingly, and she would immediately forget that problem that was upsetting her soul.

She was just as beautiful, maybe more beautiful, with that touch of maturity given by her approaching thirties. Those deep eyes, which seemed to carry all the blue Danube in them, still fascinated Manuel. Queen Amelie was glad that he was happy and she didn't inquire about the lack of a heir. It did not matter; what mattered was that they got along well with each other.

When they left the following day, on the second day of Christmas, there were no tears as before. On the contrary, Amelie told them laughing, that that week full of entertainment would be enough for her until their next visit. And she advised her son to start writing, or better said, to start fulfilling his dream from childhood.

In Sigmaringen it was colder, but the castle rooms were well heated. There Augusta's brothers gathered, too, and the parties had a youthful quality about them. Manuel was playing the piano fairly well, so that their evenings were entertaining. On New Year's Eve, there was champagne, but no fireworks. Nobody could afford that after the war, especially since the Germans had lost. They came out to watch the eternal river, which insouciantly waved its waters toward the Black Sea, uniting Sigmaringen with the Kingdom of Romania and Ferdinand I, Augusta's uncle.

It was 1920, the first year truly without war, when Europe was patching up its wounds, trying to stand. A difficult goal to attain, we would say, but not impossible. The Europeans have always been resourceful.

They returned to Fulwell Park just as cheerful as when they had left on their journey. They were planning to throw a party, a ball, to raise funds to help the victims of the war, widows and orphans. Augusta was matchless when it came to organizing those pleasant gatherings, during which she had to solicit donations for the causes they were both dedicated to. She knew how to draw attention to herself. She was beautiful, supple, impeccable, a true princess, and the English liked her and forgot where she had been born and who she was. The guests would come to Fulwell Park with all their heart, and Manuel and Augusta would add up all their purse.

Sadness pressed in upon them in February, when they received a letter from Naples. Manuel's uncle Afonso had died at almost 55. The couple embarked for France, then crossed into Italy for those solemn ceremonies. Amelie too attended the funeral. The Duke of Porto was buried in Italian soil, and Manuel promised he would strive to have his body moved to Portugal. Actually, his wife wanted also to sustain those efforts, for she was the heiress of all her husband's rights. She was an interesting and pleasant person; nobody had anything against her, and Afonso had loved her for certain, as he had given up everything for her.

Upon their return to England, Manuel wrote a long letter to the Portuguese government demanding that his uncle's body be brought to his country and buried in the Pantheon of the House of Braganza. The former King mentioned he would not accompany the deceased one, thus respecting the law of exile. Only the wife of the Duke of Porto, who had no right of succession to the throne, would go along to his country.

60

After a long wait, the government agreed to Manuel's request, and one year later, Afonso's wife brought her late husband to his native country to rest with his family members in the Braganza Pantheon. That successful action had been the first opening in the government's intransigence.

A year later, Manuel was informed and taken by surprise by Miguel II's gesture, who had given up all his rights to the throne in favor of his son, Duarte Nuno. By that act, the two branches of the Braganza House – the Constitutional one belonging to Maria II, which Manuel was part of, and the absolutist one belonging to Miguel I – joined hands and quietly reunited after many years. Manuel was happy. Since he had no heirs, the closest branch to the throne was indeed the "Miguel-ist" one. He saluted that renouncement, which also silenced the parties sustaining the two protagonists, those in the center who supported Miguel II, and those in the North who supported Manuel II. He remembered the meeting in Dover and the fact that indeed, his heir was Duarte Nuno. It had been so long since then! There had been a war, and everything taken together, good and bad, it hadn't put him down.

Following Augusta's advice, Manuel began documenting his favorite period in the history of Portugal, the Medieval era and the Renaissance, when glory reached its climax in that sunny country. He wrote with passion, accurately and with no trace of embellishment, like a true historian. He resumed his favorite sports, fencing and horseback riding, and especially tennis, where he had his beautiful Augusta as partner.

After the war ended, he lost no more competitions in Wimbledon, sporting competitions of course. Many rules changed in the aftermath of that great world war. He was no longer the only exiled person in Europe; there had been others as well, owing to the disintegration of the empires of the old continent. Many had left their countries and were now wandering anywhere but in the country they had ruled. The harshest fate struck Russia, where the drama of the tsars spread throughout the continent. Maybe it was for the better for Carlos I that he did not know his destiny, and implicitly his future, either. The Romanovs saw it every day, wondering simply: when? The Habsburgs had fallen, too. Their fame had fallen simultaneously with their black and yellow flag, and hence many new States, a whole reorganization

Thank God Portugal kept its independence, he thought to himself, pleased, as he was sitting one day in the park of his house, meditating upon the fate that a war may change in a few years. He looked within his heart and found that he was happy and didn't need anything else in the world.

The world had changed. He had to adapt to the world; he had no choice. He wanted to live in this world as long as possible next to his German princess. He had one more joy: his mother was still alive, and she wrote long letters to him, which fed his soul every single time.

CHAPTER 10

On one of the warm days of April, 1922, Manuel, with his wife and a few close friends, had gone out for a walk to enjoy the sun of London. It wasn't raining, because the sky had poured all night long. The king was enjoying taking pictures. He arranged his cameras so as to catch his friends in all kinds of poses. And it wasn't the first time. When processing them later, they were all having so much fun looking at the hilarious situations in which they were immortalized. They had taken photos of their dogs, their horses, of the park. He liked that miracle of remaining on paper for eternity.

"They are all immortal," he said, "including my cigar. Look at it here, Augusta, in the photo. I smoked it a month ago, but it still exists."

Augusta was laughing at their immortality, at the immortality of all their pets and animals and of all their guests at their parties, whom Manuel loved to photograph. They were at a tea party when a servant came in with a letter, laid on a beautiful silver tray. Manuel took it with curiosity and read it.

"It's from Miguel II. He probably has something very important to tell me. As we know, he ceded his rights to his son. Manuel took the letter and carefully read it. "Meeting in Paris! Hm.... A good opportunity to see mother, but I don't understand him anymore. Duarte Nuno is my successor, since our agreement in Dover. What is wrong? You know, Augusta, how complicated this is! The other branches without rights to the throne do not acknowledge this branch, because neither the father, nor the son was born in Portugal. Miguel I was dispossessed of all his rights, and his son and his nephew were born far from their country. I'd like this to be over! Portugal is a Republic now, and I no longer see it as a monarchy. I shall go and see what he wants now, but I think that mother is more drawing me to go on this trip."

In Paris, Amelie received him with open arms. It was warmer and more pleasant than in England.

"I advise you to acknowledge Duarte Nuno once again," she said.

"Yes, of course I will acknowledge him, even if I have to let the Parliament of the country decide his fate, for I don't have a heir."

"Yes, son, but your word carries much weight; it would be like a suggestion to the politicians," the Queen said.

"And one more interesting detail: they acknowledge me as King in exile, as if I weren't one without their acknowledgement. I have started writing about the glorious Portugal, the Portugal full of colonies and prosperity. This really concerns me. Do you know that the father of Duarte Nuno is not coming? Someone taking care of this child is coming, someone who is not my peer. I find that odd. I shall go there, don't worry. I think I'll send a representative, too. I have in mind Ornelas, to meet Countess Aldegundes de Bardi."

After the meeting, his secretary, Aires de Ornelas, conveyed to Manuel that the agreement related to Duarte Nuno was still valid and that he would be the heir, as previously set and acknowledged.

"But I have known that for a long time, from England. Anything else?" Manuel asked Ornelas.

"They want to close their newspaper, just as Your Majesty wished. But they told me that secretively."

"That is good. There will be more peace in the country," Manuel said, standing up, a sign that he had heard enough. His secretary withdrew, bowing slightly, and immediately went out the door.

"I think I have to go back to my writing, Manuel said to himself. "It's more attractive and healthful."

For as long as he stayed in Paris, his mother accompanied him to the Opera, to the theater, and on walks. He had bought a present for Augusta, which would definitely cheer her, he thought. His wife always rejoiced like a child, no matter how small and insignificant the present might be. He was thrilled by that and loved her even more. He was already missing her.

He left to return home happy, after he had taken pictures of all of Paris, as his mother put it. She was so very well accustomed to the peace of solitude. Augusta received him with love and was happy for his return, for she didn't like being alone in that country that had adopted her, too. She preferred being withdrawn most of the time when her husband was away. She waited for him to come back, so they could go out together. The dogs, the books, and the flowers in the greenhouse were enough for her.

They made a vivid impression on her through their purity. But nothing compared to her husband.

She didn't ask him anything, but she could see that that visit should not have taken place. But then time passed among seasons, social life, and her husband's writings. Manuel was writing so beautifully about Portugal, which Augusta had not seen, but could imagine from what her dear Manuel said about it. He repeated to her that there is never winter, and that the sun shines most of the time. Augusta was curious as to why there was no snow in winter, and yet that period was still called "winter." Then Manuel started laughing and gave her another finished chapter to read and share her opinions on what he had written.

When he wanted a break, he would take Augusta and their dogs and go for a walk in the paths of their wonderful park. Arm in arm, ever since they had known each other, they were fulfilling their love. They were truly happy and that was what really mattered. Fulwell Park, their beloved refuge, was their witness. Every tree moving its branches seemed to respond to them and chide them sometimes if they were not together under its branches, on a bench beneath its shadow. That was a lovely marriage, envied by many people, even if they did not have children. The couple themselves were most important.

Augusta was proud of Manuel and told him so all the time. She asked him to publish his writing, because success would show its fruit and the goal was absolutely sublime. Augusta was a romantic, just like Manuel, in fact.

At last, the first printed volume appeared and his concise and elaborate style, well founded on the documents, caught the public. He was applauded on the evening held in honor of that event, and researchers said nothing critical.

"Finally, I get to do what I like and what I was educated to do! Look, my mother is congratulating me and so is George V. That means I have to print the other parts as well. My country will come to be known everywhere through me as well. So I am useful somehow."

By the end of the third decade, Manuel had published another volume, just as well received by the critics and experts, but above all the recognition, proving to the whole world that his heart had remained at home, that Portugal was his country and that his soul was full of patriotism. He could not enter Portugal, according to the laws of 1834, but he was close to his country through his writings.

Not even the letter of Countess Aldegundes de Bardi, from 1925, made him react anymore. She was upset because the integralists had closed the newspaper, while the constitutionalists' newspaper was still alive, thereby offending the former. Thus the agreement, so frail and relative, between the two sides of the Braganza House, was broken. But Manuel was writing and knew what he would be remembered for, namely his unconditional love for his country and his people.

That year, 1930, the two of them decided to celebrate their birthday together in August after Wimbledon. Augusta turned 40, and Manuel, 41. That was a good idea, and the weather was favorable, for it did not rain at all on that day. On the lawn behind their house, their close friends had wished them many happy returns together. In the lights of the torches, the couple appeared more in love than ever. There were no fireworks at midnight – who in fact could afford that luxury? – but the torches were sufficient and more beautiful, because they lasted longer, all night long. The dogs did not get any sleep, either; they were running around, not being used to clear nights just like the days. When the festivities were over and the guests had left, the two of them lingered awhile longer on a bench.

"Manuel, this year you were "born" on my birthday, and you've become half a year younger, from March until August," Augusta said happily. "We are already growing older, but that doesn't matter. If we had peace, how marvelous that would be! You would be still writing, and I would be reading what you finish without making any sound!

"I don't feel I'm growing old, maybe only my body. You see, my soul is like at the age of twenty. Nothing prevents me from wandering far away with my thoughts or have them scattered to several places. I also have my memories. If I were twenty, I wouldn't have you, our engagement night, those fireworks over the Danube, our wedding and all our journeys so far and their memories. But it's getting chilly out here, the chill of the morning in England. I think we'd better go inside."

The two of them stood up, hand in hand, and Augusta's fresh laugh could be heard until the door closed behind them. She had been so beautiful in her simple dress, simple but very appropriate for her personality and nature.

Thus, the King let go any further thought about a prospective comeback on the throne of Portugal, calmly took care of his studies and his work. Everybody was praising him and waiting for the third volume, which he announced was in progress. Amelie, the Queen Mother, told the "writer" that she was happy for his tranquility and that she was waiting for them both to come to Paris, to be together, just the three of them. Augusta was proud that she was the first to read everything that her husband wrote, and she was on the verge of letting everyone know about that joy. King George V was thrilled, he was also reading during his spare time, but up to a limit, when he was not caught up in State affairs. He too was quite impressed by Manuel and the marriage he made with the German princess. They did not have a hundred lives ahead of them to look into each other's eyes, King George V King thought every time they saw them together.

In 1931, they went to Paris, where Amelie was extremely glad to see them again. The Queen had grown old; naturally, the years had passed for her, too, but the kindness in her eyes was still there, and that made one think of children. If she had had grandchildren, she would have spoiled them for certain, and it would have been difficult for the nannies to take them from her once beautiful arms. But she did not have grandchildren, so she spoiled her pets. She lived with a few trustworthy servants, almost alone, in fact with her memories. She was always happy when her son came to visit her, and she didn't mind when he left again. He would come back again and again, at least several times a year.

From Paris, they were to go to Sigmaringen, to Augusta's father's grave, for it had been four years since he had left the world of the living. The weather had been dull that late October. The princess had been close to her husband and easily recovered. It was like a magic charm. In truth, the Germans get over such a loss more easily; they have a certain dignity which other people do not have.

"Watch the Danube, my love! It's always here," Manuel said from the boat taking them for a walk, unknown by anyone.

They loved going for a walk all by themselves, turning into common people, and they frequently managed to do that. They gave the impression of being only a couple of young people very much in love. They stole smiles from strangers but were not recognized.

"I was born here," she whispered, thrilled, looking at the castle perched on the huge rock. "How beautiful it is, but what is more beautiful is that nobody knows who I am! I can look at it in peace."

They returned refreshed to England, and at the end of this trip, Fulwell Park was waiting for them as always. Everything was there in its place, in the long known order, unchanged by any idea of anyone. That was their home, which they adored. There, Amelie of Orleans had been born. That house connected them through so many things.

They had invited guests for New Year's Eve, but not so many as in the previous years. It was even more pleasant that way. It had snowed a little, but it soon turned into rain, to Augusta's sadness.

"You are not allowed to be sad, my dear, because otherwise you will be like this during the whole year of 1932. It did snow a little, though, of course not as much as in Sigmaringen, but you should be pleased."

"Yes, you are right, forgive me, darling! I was hoping it would last, but that was impossible. And now let's go, the guests are waiting for us!"

All their guests spent the night in their home, and the breakfast on the 1st of January, 1932 was a joyful one and quite animated. They would all leave the next day. Everyone who was invited to the home of the King of Portugal was always enchanted. Wine was always of the best vintage, and the steaks were truly a delicacy. The princess was a charming hostess, and age did not steal away that rare quality of hers.

After the guests left, the house was empty. Stillness seemed strange after their house had resounded with so much joy during those days. But they had to get used to the quiet. Manuel was striving to finish the last part of his writing and spent most of his time in his study, while Augusta had found an occupation, namely taking care of the plants in the greenhouse. It was very relaxing for her and she enjoyed it. When they met, each of them would tell the other what they had been doing in the meantime, and then they would go for a walk, have lunch or dinner, and thus the days passed.

Manuel had had a delightful birthday cake on his birthday. Augusta asked that they write "43" on it.

"That old I am? Are you sure?" the King asked his wife, laughing.

"Yes, of course. I am 42 this year, and I will also write my age on my cake, just like I did for you! I'll show them I don't care that time passes by."

"Well done, Augusta!" Manuel answered her and lit a cigar. "Don't let anything darken your forehead. Any age is beautiful in its own way. My mother is also beautiful, and a lot of years have passed by in her life."

After dinner, they took a walk on the bank of the Thames, hand in hand, as always. The days were getting longer, and the cold had receded a bit.

In mid-June, Manuel finished the last part of his book on Portugal, which he hadn't seen for over twenty years. He needed only to talk to his publisher, Margery Winters, and everything would work out. Before that, he wanted to go to Wimbledon, to that important tennis tournament that he never missed. Most of the time, he went there with Augusta, ceremoniously greeting everyone they knew in the arena. He was enchanted by the sport that he also practiced, in fact, very well, and Augusta was a perfect partner for him.

But on the 1st of July, Augusta had to pay an urgent visit and did not accompany him to Wimbledon. She left him with his male friends on a "men's day out." The starting time for the game arrived and the group of friends was already seated. Manuel was happy like a child that his favorite player won the game. Then they all left and had lunch by themselves, and afterwards they went their own ways. Manuel was not expecting his wife until the following day in the evening, so he had to do something to pass the time. He went to the greenhouse and caressed the small plants that Augusta had planted. She was better than he at gardening. Probably it was that womanly touch.

He felt lonely, but he knew that after that night, Augusta would be with him again. He went outside and decided to sit on the bench and go to sleep late at night. He smoked cigar after cigar, so that time would pass faster. He went to bed after midnight, already saying: "Today!" and thinking about his wife. He went to sleep after the servant prepared his bath, which he always preferred hot.

But something made him feel dizzy, maybe from the water, he thought, and then his doctor would also say that to him sometimes. He felt his throat get dry and got up to get some water. He drank as if it had been the first time in his life, but the dryness wouldn't leave him. Probably he had been sitting in a drought, plus the fatigue and the smoking – they all came together.

He called the servant, asking him to get him a pill to soothe his throat. The man quickly brought him the medicine and left. The pill was of no use for him. He shouted again, realizing that it sounded as if it weren't his voice, as if it had hoarsened all of a sudden. The good servant entered at once, and Manuel explained to him that the pain wouldn't go away and that he'd better get a doctor. He was worried because Augusta wasn't there with him. If she had been there, he was sure he wouldn't have had that sore throat. His personal doctor came at once and found Manuel coughing, talking in a hoarse whisper.

"I feel I'm suffocating, doctor! Do something!" The King gasped.

The doctor placed his hand on Manuel's throat, then looked at him; he felt his chest and sighed. He could feel the swelling right under his very hands.

"Why are you sighing? You don't think that ...," Manuel did not go on uttering the word. "I've smoked too much and I'm terribly thirsty."

The doctor prepared him a pain killer, and the King appeared to relax. Toward morning, the doctor and the servant were awakened from their armchairs by the rattles of the former King who was suffocating. The doctor whispered to the servant to call a priest, and the man staggering to his feet, then ran. Manuel was aware, even if his brain was not receiving enough air. The attack was in its early phase.

"Tell me the truth, doctor," Manuel said, in a whisper, then pulled the doctor toward him with his last strength.

"Your Majesty, what you suffer from can be neither controlled nor prevented. It is an unexpected inflammation of the vocal cords, a swelling of the larynx, with a very rapid and dramatic development."

"I shall die suffocated by my own throat?" The King asked, incredulous, his chest rattling.

"It is called a glottic spasm, Your Majesty. There is nothing that can be done about it. The medicine is useless. Today you feel good, and tomorrow you suffocate."

The pastor at the St. James Church came quickly with the servant next to him.

"Father, listen to what my the doctor is telling me," Manuel gasped, in a lisping and sibilant voice. "Yesterday I was fine and today I'm dying while my wife is on the continent. She must be told!"

The priest was left with his patient for a short while. The words of the priest somehow helped Manuel, though he was still in pain and needed air. He was struggling to breathe as little as he possibly could, then he would be calm for a few seconds, and afterwards he would resume, even more tragically. That went on for a couple of hours. And yet, he was still a young man.

He died all alone, just as he had ruled Portugal. He passed away before Augusta came back home.

"God, what have I done? Why did I go away from him," she cried, when she discovered him dead. "If I had stayed with him, none of this would have happened. He was my soul mate. What am I going to do now? How will I break this to Queen Amelie?"

A priest helped her, and soon everybody learned the news officially. His friends, with whom he had spent the whole previous day, were the most shocked. That attack had been fast and merciless.

Thus the last king of Portugal passed away, all alone, shouting voicelessly for Augusta, and leaving the unpublished volume to posterity for their edification.

Upon learning the news, his friend, King George V became dejected. He could not understand the doctors' helplessness. Today you are fine, then your throat swells, and then you suffocate. It could have happened to anyone.

Princes and kings gathered to say goodbye to Manuel, to that family so tragically burdened. The Queen Mother and Augusta, in mourning, were waiting for Manuel to be transferred to the Westminster Cathedral, for the Requiem Mass. George V had promised that afterwards

Manuel's body would be repatriated, something requested by the church St. Charles Borremec in Weybridge. The new president of the republic, Antonio de Oliveira Salazar, gave his consent for the King to come back to his country, and have a national funeral. He was to rest forever next to his relatives, in the Pantheon of their family, where preparations were already made.

Those who wanted to say goodbye to the King could do so for several weeks in the church where he was lying in state. Amelie decided to stay near Augusta, until Manuel's body was placed on the ship going to Portugal. They knew that the royal family was not allowed to accompany him, so Manuel was to leave all alone, to everyone's shocked disbelief.

In early August, 1932, the English ship HMS Concord was headed up the Tejo River, bringing the body that the Portuguese were waiting for. From time to time, one of the ship's cannons would fire as a sign of respect. All the churches in the capital were ringing their bells continuously, which was touching and shattering at the same time. They were waiting for the body to be taken off the ship, the same place where in 1908, the whole family had come down from their vacation in Vila Vicosa: the trade square. One could see the coffin covered with flowers and draped with the Portuguese monarchal flag. In the square, all the important officials of the country waited for the young King. The Army, all in parade dress, but wearing the sign of mourning, waited for an order to present arms. People were screaming, crying and jostling, to the displeasure of the police officers who had to ensure order.

The English let down the coffin and the flowers; they saluted Portugal one more time and then left to go back home. Manuel was put on a cannon carriage, with flowers all around him. They held a Mass for him; they presented arms, and they sang the Portugal national anthem. Slowly, the convoy with Portugal's last king crossed the streets among cries, ovations, and flowers thrown from the sidewalks. The balconies of the public institutions had been ornate in mourning, and the flags flew at half-mast.

Everything ended with the arrival of the body at the family Pantheon, where he was interred at the set place. There they held another Mass, and then the ceremonies were over, with the flowers covering everything.

In Fulwell Park, women were despondently thinking about their incapacity to do anything. They hoped that Salazar would keep his promise. Augusta had already started packing her things, for she knew the will of her husband and she was preparing to go back home, to her native land Baden-Wurttemberg. Amelie was also contemplating the idea of leaving. There, everything aggrieved her, even the fact that she had first seen daylight under that very roof.

"It's better that it be sold. It has no more value without Manuel," Amelie said, disconsolate.

"Yes, I agree. I wouldn't know what to do all by myself anyway, in this big house without him," Augusta added.

After Amelie left for Paris, Augusta remained only long enough to gather her things in peace. The Portuguese Government had not imposed a date on her, but they were the masters, the owners. She had gathered several cherished things, which she had carefully packed, to go to her country. On her last evening there, she stayed in the garden in the lovely weather to say goodbye to everything, to the greenhouse, to the trees, to the fall that would come soon.

The next day, a car and a truck moved slowly toward Baden. They were to cross the water to France, then slowly go to lands far, far away from her love, from their love.

The Salazar Government kept its promise, and by selling all of Manuel's goods, established the Foundation of the House of Braganza, thus observing the wish of the former king. As a sign, Fulwell Park was demolished to make room for the city's expansion; only the old St. James church still remains, with its stained glass window with the emblem of the Portuguese Royal House, a sign of the passing through there of some famous and wonderful people.

The third volume of his book, which Manuel had happily and wholeheartedly worked on, was published after his death, thus crowning the success of the other two published while he was alive. Duarte Nuno remained his heir, becoming the 23rd Duke of Braganza and head of the Portuguese Royal House. Thus, Miguel supporters won, for their rights, lost because of the reckless actions of Portuguese King Miguel I, had been restored.

The End

18.03.2013

The following novels written by the same author were published also by Infarom Publishing:

"Destine" (Destinies);
"Lucia; Tatăl meu este soarele şi mama mea este luna" (Lucia; My father is the sun, and my mother is the moon);
"A Butterfly with Burning Wings".